J. O. Barrett, J. M. Peebles

The Gadarene: or, Spirits in Prison

J. O. Barrett, J. M. Peebles

The Gadarene: or, Spirits in Prison

ISBN/EAN: 9783744784368

Printed in Europe, USA, Canada, Australia, Japan

Cover: Foto ©Andreas Hilbeck / pixelio.de

More available books at **www.hansebooks.com**

THE

GADARENE:

OR,

SPIRITS IN PRISON.

By J. O. BARRETT and J. M. PEEBLES.

"Try the Spirits whether they are of God; for many false prophets have
gone out into the world."—*Apostle John.*

BOSTON:
COLBY AND RICH,
BANNER OF LIGHT OFFICE,
9 Montgomery Place.
1874.

DEDICATED

TO

THE PURE IN HEART.

DEAR READER:

We have only briefly to say: That we write this book from a sense of solemn duty, indifferent alike to encomium and criticism. It is fact we are after; and the truth we mean to speak at any hazard. The world is full of "seducing spirits and doctrines of devils speaking lies in hypocrisy." Our mission is to expose them; explain the canses and suggest the remedies.

AUTHORS.

INDEX

OF CHAPTERS AND SUBDIVISIONS.

CHAPTER IV.

CHAPTER V.

CHAPTER VI.

CHAPTER VII.

CHAPTER VIII.

CHAPTER IX.

CHAPTER X.

CHAPTER XI.

CHAPTER XII.

ANALYTICAL INDEX.

THE GADARENE.

CHAPTER I.

MORAL GOOD AND EVIL.

THE common consciousness of the race admits a standard of moral rectitude. This is the transcendent law of humanity. Protagoras was a cunning sophist; Socrates, a philosopher. "Man is the measure of all things," said Protagoras; "and, as men differ, there can be no absolute truth." "Man is the measure of all things," replied Socrates; "but descend deeper into his personality, and you will find that underneath all varieties there is a ground of *steady truth*. Men differ, but men also agree: they differ as to what is fleeting; they agree as to what is eternal. Difference is the region of opinion; Agreement is the region of Truth: let us endeavor to penetrate that region."

Pseudo-philosophers tell us there is no moral evil in the universe—only a graded good. Is a lie a lower degree of truth? hate a lower degree of love? rape a lower degree of chastity?   To enunciate is to reveal the hideousness of such reasoning.

The objection is mooted, that what we regard as good to-day may be our evil to-morrow.   Admitted on the score of progress.   But is moral distinction thus annulled?   Do we not again have our contrasts—what we like and dislike—what to us is good and what evil?   A simple fact in science—often used in argument against the existence of evil—will cover the whole ground in plain sight: There is heat in cold.   True, but does this destroy our mental consciousness of the distinction between heat and cold?   Do not our sensations test them?   Divide and subdivide infinitesimally the two conditions.   They are still related to each other as opposites.   But, really, what has all this to do with *moral* qualities?   The logician does not connect moral evil or moral good with fire and ice, stocks and stones—only by association; of themselves they have no intrinsic morality.

None will dispute that the brain is the organ of the human mind.   Phrenology, received into the pantheon of the sciences, admits man to be a moral being, having moral faculties.   Moral being implies moral law, and moral law implies not only conscience and freedom, but moral government and compensation.   Conscience in connection with moral judgment ever prompts to the right; but the reflective organs in connection with moral consciousness, must ever determine what the right is.   This applies to every scale of human life.

" Green apples are good," says a writer—" good in

their place as the ripened ones of October." The proposition is a bald sophism. Neither green nor ripened apples are good. No *moral* quality inheres in apples. They are neither good nor evil, because moral qualities pertain to moral beings—not to unconscious fruit or blind forces.

Good and evil are *moral* conditions, each positive according as it becomes the leading force in purpose or quality of character. Hate, that stirs the murderous intent, lifts the hand and sends the dagger into its victim for a selfish end, is just as positive as love equally earnest in forgiving the murderer, under the law of reform. Malice, that, with cold foresight and determination, plots to pursue innocence and gratify fiendish instincts, is just as positive as mercy that unfalteringly weeps over trespass and forgets the wrong.

Nero's hellish fiddling over the crackling flames of burning Rome—was it good? Will you affirm that the deed steeled those Christians to greater vigilance, and here is the good? As if the contrast of moral righteousness, thus provoked to activity, were the apologist for such human malignancy! There stands the bare fact—*murder!*—was it good?

But here comes the "old *saw:*" "Who made Nero? Did he not act true to his conditions?"

What do you mean by conditions? Do you mean that conditions compelled the murderous act? that conditions *alone* mechanically *forced* the fiddling? If this is the position of the objector, it virtually unmans Nero and transforms him into a human-shaped piece of mechanism, minus volition of will and a moral nature.

As a Spiritual Philosopher, asking this question— Who made Nero?—you deny the fundamental principle of your belief. As put, it implies a personal God who fashions arbitrarily as the potter does the clay. The very implication is a charge against a personal God for the existence of such a monster. If, with honest concession, you affirm that his parents or preceding parents, together with his after surroundings, manufactured Nero's life into such a mold, you have only shifted the responsibility, making culpability lodge where it more naturally belongs. So there is, argue as you will, an evil still, and a moral responsibility somewhere.

As God, the Absolute Energy, or Impersonal Spirit, governs the Universe by inflexible law, the divine effort must ceaselessly tend to the mitigation of evil—not as excusing, but as overcoming evil with good. An eminent New-Church writer affirms this: "It is therefore obvious that the condition of the whole, of all the human race considered as one, must be constantly and eternally improving. * * * As the heavens grow in their perfection, the earths receive through them more fully of the divine life, for the heavens are the mediums through which that life passes; and thus improvement, eternal progress, is the constant law of the universe."

Character is the reflex action of soul-affection. "As a man thinketh, so is he." Those who have but little sense of moral responsibility are quite indifferent to moral conduct. When a man pronounces judgment favorable to vice, is he not to be judged by his own judgment? Does not a careless apology, or argument for evil, implicate one as engulphed in the love of evil?

The higher the moral altitude attained, the more exquisitely keen are the soul's distinctions between good and evil; and the more intense the pain at the discovery of the least moral taint upon the character. Not that such an individual's charity is less for the erring, but that his capacity for weighing the sufferings incidentally resulting from the commission of evils, is more sensitive and tender in sympathy, and better adjusted to the absolute relations of justice and love.

ANCIENT MORALS.

The distinction between good and evil, right and wrong, has ever marked the ages of human civilization, showing a common moral inheritance here which we of the nineteenth century can but cherish as the way to heaven. The testimony of the seers and moralists of ancient days, whose lives were self-abnegating and whitened by adversities in the struggle to attain the highest and best of character, unmistakably shows that man, in all ages, has discerned our law, requiring that moral evil must be overcome with the merciless rigor that a wise man removes a disease or physical evil from his body.

From the great ocean of moral law in the past, let

2

us glean a few jewels, and learn not only charity, but purity, as the law of God written upon our hearts:

"My doctrine is simple and easy to understand. It consists only in having the heart right, and in loving one's neighbor as one's self."—*Confucius.*

"Generosity, liberality, and benevolence, are more conformable to human nature, than the love of pleasure, of riches, or even of life."—*Cicero.*

"Whosoever wishes to be happy must attach himself to justice, and walk humbly and modestly in her steps."—*Plato.*

"Do what you know to be right without expecting any glory from it."—*Demophiles.*

"The virtuous man buries in silence his good deeds."—*Plutarch.*

In Plutarch, and the yet later writers, Seneca and Epictetus, the like sentiments are found. Marcus Aurelius, the philosophic Emperor, compares the wise and humane soul to a "spring of pure and sweet water, which, though the passer-by may curse it, continues to offer him a draught to assuage his thirst; and even if he cast into it mire and filth, hastens to reject it, and flows on pure and undisturbed." We are also reminded of the equally beautiful image in the Oriental apologue of the sandal tree, which, in the moment when it falls before the woodman's stroke, "gives its fragrance to the axe which smites it with death."

And so the following Pythagorean and Brahminic precepts drift the grateful soul toward the same safe harbor of rest:

" Every soul is a repository of principles. In it centres the good of good things, and to it there clings the evil of things depraved."

" Bodies are cleansed by water; the mind is purified by truth; the vital spirit, by theology and devotion; the understanding, by clear knowledge."

" The resignation of all pleasures is far better than the attainment of them."

" The organs being strongly attached to the sensual delights, cannot so effectually be restrained by avoiding incentives to pleasure as by a constant pursuit of divine knowledge."

" Iniquity, once committed, fails not of producing fruit to him who wrought it, if not in his own person, yet in his sons; or, if not in his sons, yet in his grandsons."

The five commandments of the Buddhist religion which was established centuries before the Christian era, and counts among its adherents more millions than any other church, are these:

" 1. Thou shalt not kill.   2. Thou shalt not steal. 3. Thou shalt not commit adultery, or any impurity. 4. Thou shalt not lie.   5. Thou shalt not intoxicate thyself with drink."

And we would reckon in this same category of moral credit all that Christianity contains of the good.

" Eye hath not seen, nor ear heard, neither have entered into the heart of man the things which God hath prepared for them that love him."

" The recollection of one upward hour," says Percival, "hath more in it to tranquilize and cheer the darkness of despondency, than years of gayety and pleasure."

· Our transcendent law ever in vogue, what is the moral profit of arguing in favor of a sophism which the ages of human wisdom reject?

ARE THERE EVIL SPIRITS?

That man has a conscious existence in another life is demonstrated by the aspirations of his higher nature, by the logic of universal growth, by the testimony of the ages, by the tangible evidences of the spiritual phenomena.

The spectral analysis rests upon the now established fact, that matter of a nature common to that of the earth, and subject to its laws, exists throughout the stellar universe. What is thus true in a physical sense is true in a moral. As atom is conjoined with atom, as ether is composite, giving forth by motion its innate life, and light, and color, and transformation, so is the relation of mind with mind, allied telegraphically with all worlds, and the inhabitants of all worlds, intimately here as the physical body with its spiritual. As youth bears upon manhood, and thence manhood upon old age, so does the earth life bear upon the future character of the immortal spirit. As no physical force is lost, but only transferred, so no moral force can be neutralized by transitions from earthly to heavenly residences. Nature knows no spasms. A sudden leap from vice to virtue, from folly to wisdom, contrary to life's process of development, would be equivalent to annihilation. Only the coarsest logic will affirm that chemical changes of body will produce a moral regeneration. They may arrest or remove obstructions, like medicines, but moral cures, or growths, are the results of spirit influx and culture.

Death, the dropping of the garment in which the spirit has lived, is, in the sense of change, continuously operative; but does this change moral character? Are we better for wearing off a little epidermis by the toils of life? Are we to-day sinners, but, having had a night's sleep, are we angels on the morrow? Does a walk through a college transfer a boor into a philosopher? If the deaths, or wastes of the body, thus far, have wrought no sequential regeneration, how can a future death do it, since it is the same in physical ratio as already experienced? If the theory of the Old School Universalists were true, that death regenerates, why not at once blow out the brains and sip the sweets of paradise? and enjoy what the poet sung of the Nazarene's betrayer:

> "Judas, with a cord,
> Outstripped his Lord,
> And got to heaven first!"

The same clairvoyant and phenomenal evidences that prove the existence of spirits, prove the existence of evil, or unregenerate spirits. By the immutable law of spiritual gravity, these are here—here in the spirit world that heaves and laves all around us like an

ocean of ether. In old speculative India, in mystic
Egypt, in sunny Syria (birthplace of the Old and New
Testaments), in Persia among the star-gazers, in classic
Greece and opulent Rome, among the stern Scandinavians, sable Africans, South Sea Islanders, and wild
Indians, together with the personal experiences of
millions of Spiritualists in the present time, we have
the same chain of testimony, the same willing, or
unwilling, witnesses to the existence of evil spirits and
their power over mortals.

The wilderness of proof substantiating this position
almost staggers us. We are at a loss what to reject
from the mountainous pile of evidences which the
accumulating ages have developed for the startled
inspector.

In a recent pamphlet, entiled "The Spiritual Philosophy *versus* Diabolism," the author attempts to argue
away the perils of *infestation* on the hypothesis that
"intelligence in the higher life so controls the law of
intercourse of spirits with men in the flesh, that the
evil disposed are restrained of this intercourse."

This is virtually making a higher plane of spirits a
police institution! The author says: "No villain exists
in the spirit world but who has a master there—one
who is adapted to him, and can cast over him such a
psychological influence as to restrain him at his will.
This determines the subjection of the evil minded to
control, in spirit life, and such control as robs them of
the power to do the injury that is in their hearts to do
to mortals and spirits."

What better is this than earth's slavery revamped in the spirit world? The force of such a police cannot, of course, regenerate the wicked, but only restrain them, as in a prison. The arbitration of angels must be a fruitless business in those courts of higher law. We prefer to be excused from the office of watching devils, as picket guards in paradise. Attending to such business in this world is not considered a very exalted profession. It is just as possible for the evil minded to communicate through their thought and affection as the reverse class; the law being the same. Even if arbitrarily restrained, the peril is by no means shut off. So long as evil continues, even if the perpetrators are imprisoned, the spiritual part will act and go forth, seeking its own. Arbitrary restraint never regenerates.

The common plea mooted by this class of reasoners is, that, as God is good, "His imperative will" would never permit "the depravity of one sphere to be propagated to a lower." By parity of reasoning, God, being good, He would never permit depravity to exist at all. Evil does exist in this world, and this of itself overthrows this begging philosophy. Coming to our senses, the point is this: We are in the universe, subject to the influences of mind from all possible sources, above and below, whose temptations and invitations test our strength and grade us, up or down, according to our innate affection and practice.

This, attributed to William Denton, is decidedly pointed: "The miser returns cursing the fatal appetite

which binds him in the metalic chain forged by his own
avarice; the sensualist lives in the agonizing retrospect
of lost delights, for which the nature of spiritual existence furnishes no satisfaction."

Some of our prominent Spiritualists have taken the
ground in their works impliedly averse to the continuance of evil beyond this life, maintaining that death
is a "sieve," sifting out gross substances or adhering
contamination, leaving the spirit innately pure. The
idea is pleasant; and how much *more* pleasant, if our
birth into this world were a "sieve," and all of us were
holy.

In Mr. Davis' *Diakka*, a stirring work, he logically
traces the ratio of worlds, and admits all we claim—
that there are spirits "morally deficient and affection-
ately unclean"—a good round million of them residing
in the constellation Draco Major — whose chief business in our world is "jugglery and trickery, witticisms,
invariably victimizing others — secretly tormenting
mediums, causing them to exaggerate in speech, and
to falsify by acts; unlocking and unbolting the street
doors of your bosom and memory; pointing your feet
into wrong paths; and far more. Nevertheless, the
good physicians of love and ministers of truth labor
among the Diakka * * till all are reached and
delivered from the dense wilderness of discord."

In a recent work, entitled the "Masterion," the
author says: "If spirits are wicked, we should know
it. If our kindred in immortality, our fathers, mothers,
sisters, brothers, aunts, uncles, and cousins, have degen-

erated, or have been denuded of common sense, as a consequence of their transition to another condition of existence, then certainly it behooves us to make our stay upon earth as long as possible; nor should we yearn to know of a state of being which degrades our happiness, or bemeans our intelligence. * * * No, no; such opinions are as ficticious as the fleeting wind. We may simplify the honor, the goodness of the Divine Being by circumlocution in thought and expression; may barter away our joy and hope in a raid of words upon the godliness of spirits because they *rap* their notes of warning to the world; because they tip tables and make mock faces to establish the fact of their existence and prove their identity."

These writers who expect all the heavens to be clean, though the earth be foul, are like children who estimate spirits, as they did mortals, to be perfect, on the principle that "distance lends enchantment to the view." A closer contact with the people of both worlds, evolving conflicts and sorrows, tones such fancies to stern fact—that evil is, and we must overcome it to be angels indeed. What means this moral sentiment that sounds the deeps of our characteristic worth—" He that overcometh shall inherit all things?" Does it not cite to what we feel is true, that there is temptation to resist and good to attain? and *when* such a conquest is gained, that the victors, whether they are our relatives or not, on this side or the other, are ministrants of holy services?

Such writers ever argue the non-existence of falses

3

in the other world, because it is not like God! As if
the Divine were any more there than here! This *begging* for universal purity of the All-Pure is a sign of
a deficiency in the devotee. It dates from the defunct
dogma of an organized personal Deity, who, being
infinitely good, could not create evil. What is the use
to build on fancy? The unsubdued, the unbalanced,
the selfish, the oppressive—look at these as facts, right
in the face, and fight the battle of life like a moral
hero. This were far better. Stoical Philosophy never
grasps the problems of life as they are. This making
a *personal* God responsible! Rid the bewildered mind
of the *personality*, and this *ignis fatuus* vanishes into
thin air. Consider God as the *esse* of things, impersonal, subject like us to law, over us, in us, of us; and
that as we use or abuse our privileges, so is our weal
or woe; then have we *begun* to know something of the
necessity of "overcoming evil with good."

CHRYSALIS OF THE SPIRIT.

The spiritual man lays aside the physical body at
death, as the butterfly does its chrysalis. As the chaff
envelopes the wheat, and the pulp of the wheat envelopes the germ, so the physical body envelopes the
spiritual body, and this in turn centres or holds the
eternal principle which we call *spirit*. Death is but
the severing of the outer envelope—the physical body;
and it can no more change the moral character than
the dropping of chaff can change the nature of wheat.
The office of death, therefore, is simply the emanci-

pation that affords the liberty of spiritual growth. It
is the ever-attendant angel of progress; but progress
itself is the tenure of life—life's unfoldings. It is not
a " sieve," as by comparison is vaguely used, straining
out human imperfections; but the dismantling of
earth's garment that the spirit may clothe itself anew
according to its moral altitude attained by growth
incident to obedience to all the laws of its being.

All moral acts pertain to the intellectual and spirit
ual, and not to the body except medially. Is it the
foot that sins when treading on forbidden grounds?
the hand that steals? Are not these, rather, the implements of conscious force operating in and by them?
Without this force, or spirit, man is but a corpse, and
a corpse never violates law. The dogma that a
debauched sensualist, steeped in crime, crimsoned in
blood, principled in life-long evils, is not the same
man—the vicious spirit—when first awakened to consciousness in the future life, finds no parallel in this
life's experiences, in moral philosophy, or the teachings
of angels.

Everything physical has its counterpart in the spiritual. The physical body is but the soul's instrument
of use for a season. All sensations, all thought, reason,
moral responsibility, pertain to soul—the *inner man*.
When the twin brother of life—*death*—puts its frosty
seal upon the forehead, fortunes and all else are left
behind, save our unmasked selves. Rank and honors
avail nothing " over there." Even reputation clings
to us no more. Stripped of staff and scrip, we enter

the next state of existence the real men and women we *are*, bearing with us the plans, purposes, achievements, and deeds done, as records. These determine the commencement of future destinies.

This an unreal, that is a real life; this a shadowy, that is a substantial existence of activity and progression. Swedenborg tells us he frequently met "new-born spirits, that could not believe they had died." Their bodies, forms, limbs, were perfect in shape. Everything was real—familiar even, only more etherialized. And then their affections, their attractions, being earthly, they still lingered in and around their mortal homes.

CHAPTER II.

DEMONS AND GODS.

THE terms *gods, lords, angels, demons, spirits*, were used interchangeably by Egyptian, Phœnician, Persian, and the more ancient Grecian writers. This understood, much of the mysticism connected with God and Jehovah, Lord and Angel, as used by theologians, is cleared away. In the Old Testament we read: "In the beginning Gods (Elohim, plural) created the heaven and the earth." Hesiod has a poem entitled Theogonia, giving the "generation of the gods." "In the book of Moses," says that learned church authority, Calmet, "the name of God is often given to the *angels.* * * * Princes, magistrates, and great men are called gods. If a slave is desirous to continue with his master, he shall be brought to the gods. The Lord (an exalted angel) is seated amidst the gods, and judges with them."

The testimony of the truly eminent Philo Judæus, relative to the identity of *god, lord, angel, spirit, etc.*, is exceedingly important. We quote from Yonge's translation: "Those (referring to gods) of the most divine nature are utterly regardless of any situation on earth, but are raised to a greater height, and placed in the ether itself, being of the purest possible character,

(29)

which those among the Greeks that have studied philosophy, call heroes and demons, and which Moses, giving them a most felicitous appellation, calls angels, acting, as they do, the part of ambassadors and messengers. Therefore, if you look upon souls and demons and angels as things differing indeed in name, but as meaning in reality one and the same thing, you will thus get rid of the heaviest of all evils—superstition. For as people speak of good demons and bad demons, so do they speak of good and bad souls; and also of some angels as being by their title worthy ambassadors * * * from God to men, being sacred and inviolable guardians; others as being unholy and unworthy. Hence, the Psalmist David speaks of the 'operation of evil angels.'"

In harmony with the above, from a different source, yet in confirmation of the same general idea, we quote from the third volume of Plato, by Burges, Trinity College, Cambridge: "They are demons, because prudent and learned. * * * Hence, poets say well, who say that when a good man shall have reached his end, he receives a mighty destiny and honor, and becomes a demon according to the appellation of prudence."

Concurring with the general belief of those ages, the Grecian poet Hesiod, in his "Works and Days," says:

> "But when concealed had destiny this race,
> Demons there were, called holy upon earth,
> Good, ill-averters, and of men the guard."

Plato, in the Timœus, says: "That between God and man are the *daimones*, or spirits, who are always near us, though commonly invisible to us, and know all our thoughts. They are intermediates between gods and men, and their function is to interpret and convey to the gods what comes from men, and to men what comes from the gods."

In Plato's "Apology and Republic," (pages 31 and 40, book ten) that great master Grecian says: "The demons often direct man in the quality of guardian spirits, in all his actions, as witness the demon of Socrates. * * * There are two kinds of men. One of these, through aptitude, will receive the illuminations of divinity, and the other, through inaptitude, will subject himself to the power of avenging demons."
* * * They (the poets) do not compose by art, but through a divine power; since, if they knew how to speak by art upon the subject correctly, they would be able to do so upon all others. On this account, a deity has deprived them of their senses, and employs them as his ministers and oracle singers, and divine prophets, in order that, when we hear them, we may know it is not they, to whom sense is not present, who speak what is valuable, but the *God* himself who speaks, and through them addresses us. We are not to doubt about those beautiful poems being not human, but divine, and the work, not of men, but of gods; and that the poets are nothing else but interpreters of the gods, (that is,

spirits,) possessed by whatever deity they may happen
to be."

The Kabala, containing a comprehensive account of
magic among the Jews, teaches that, besides the angels,
"there is a middle race of beings usually called *Ele-
mentary Spirits.* These are the dregs, or lowest of
the spiritual orders. Their head is Asmodeus. They
are of a wicked disposition, deceive men, and delight
in evil."

TESTIMONY OF THE DOCTORS.

Egyptian Jews, most German rationalists, and not a
few Universalists, who theorize outside of facts and
the recently well-established principles of psychologic
science, regard "demons," *all* the spiritual beings of
the spirit world, as perfect and holy. The orthodox,
who believe in a semi-omnipotent devil—sectarists, the
superstitious and ignorant, consider all demons "evil
spirits," that is, irredeemable, fallen angels. The truth
lies between these extremes. Demons are simply the
immortalized men of the other life—*spirits*, occupying
various planes or mansions in that "house not made
with hands"—the temple of the Eternal.

"*Demons* were of two kinds: the one were the souls
of good men, which, upon the departure from the body,
were called *heroes*, were afterwards raised to the dig-
nity of *demons*, and subsequently to that of *gods*."—
Kitto.

Demon, "the spirit of a dead man."—*Jones.*

Demon, "a spirit, either angel or fiend."—*Cudworth.*

"Demons and gods were considered the same in Greece."—*Grote.*

"The heathen authors allude to possession by a demon (or by a god, for they employ the two words with little or no distinction) as a thing of no uncommon occurrence."—*Archbishop Whately.*

"All Pagan antiquity affirms that from Titan and Saturn, the poetic progeny of Cœlus and Terra, down to Æsculapius, Proteus, and Minos, all their *divinities* were *ghosts of dead men*, and were so regarded by the most erudite of the Pagans themselves."—*Alexander Campbell.*

"The notion of demons, or the souls of the dead, having power over living men, was *universally* prevalent among the heathen of those times, and believed by many Christians."—*Dr. Lardner.*

Worcester, in his synonymes, says: "Demon is sometimes used in a good sense; as, 'The demon of Socrates, or the demon of Tasso'"—and then, to illustrate, quotes from that fine author, Addison: "My good *demon*, who sat at my right hand during the course of this vision," etc.

That learned *savant*, Cardan, honored with the friendship of Gregory XIII., says: "No man was ever great in any art or action, that did not have a demon to aid him."

Traverse Oldfield entertained the idea that the Greek *daimon* was nothing but the nervous principle; and is not this a close approximation to the office of spirits? The "nervous principle" is certainly the implement

of the gods, and can be used for good or evil, as the
will of the spirit determines.

Aware that the demoniacal possessions of the New
Testament have been the subject of much discussion
for centuries by the learned, we present certain logical
facts for candid consideration. The position of "Rationalists" and "Universalists" that these demons
were nothing more than lunacy, epilepsy, and sundry
diseases, must seem to every sound thinker exceedingly
weak and illogical.

If *demons* were simply natural, physical diseases,
was it not a matter of the highest importance that
Jesus should have undeceived his cotemporaries, Jews
and Greeks, upon this vital point, thus correcting the
erroneous and pernicious philosophy of the age? But
he did not in a single instance. To say, as some have,
he accommodated himself to the prevailing notions of
the times, is simply to say, in the language of another,
"He who came to bear witness to the truth, accommodated himself to a *lie*." Suppose we were to substitute
diseases for *demons*, in the scriptural accounts. Take,
as an illustration, Mark xvi: 9, reading, "Now when
Jesus was risen, * * * he appeared first to Mary
Magdalen, out of whom he had cast seven devils"—
daimonia, demons. Who, with any scholarly reputation at stake, would assume the responsibility of giving
us such a rendering and exegesis as the following:
"Out of whom he had cast seven devils"—that is,

seven diseases, lunacy, lumbago, dyspepsia, rheumatism, colic, pneumonia, and the measles!

These obsessing *demons* could not have been diseases and lunatics alone, because they conversed intelligently with Jesus, uttering propositions undeniably correct, and such as were happily adapted to the occasion. On the other hand, Jesus addressed these *demons* — spirits — as thinking, conscious individualities, and commanded them, as beings distinct from the obsessed or psychologized parties, to leave.

CHAPTER III.

WHETHER matter be gaseous or gross, it is one and the same in essence. Dissolve the granite into its original elements, summarily they are still granite. Form is only the crystallization of primal ether—what an ingrained law constructs.

> " The scheme of things with all the sights you see
> Are only pictures of the things that be.
> What you call matter, is but as the sheath
> Shaped ever as bubbles are by spirit-breath.
> The mountains are but firmest clouds of earth,
> Still changing to the breath that gave them birth.
> Spirit aye shapeth matter into view,
> As music wears the form it passes through.
> Spirit is lord of substance, matter's sole
> First cause, and forming power, and final goal. .,

It was a doctrine of Leucippus and Democrites— the masters of Epicurus—several centuries before the Christian era, that matter is composed of invisible, but indestructible corpuscles, diffused through all space; that they are endowed with shape and motion; that they have an evolution and differentiation by means of relationship; that a central principle, or instinctive intelligence, causes these phenomena. Descartes, Leibnitz and other modern thinkers, reproducing the ancient philosophers for a basis, have discovered by closer analysis the chemical and ethereal constituents of these corpuscles; that by their own innate, affinitive and repellent motions, each evolves around itself a refined sphere, which, blended together, constitutes a universal medium that was suspected by the ancients.

A UNIVERSAL ELASTIC MEDIUM.

This medium is elastic, so attenuated as to elude our physical senses, or even the spectroscope which recognizes the most infinitesimal gaseous atoms. It performs for the universal worlds in space what our nervous system does for its grosser body. It transmits the impressions of solar light, heat, magnetism, electricity, and atinic force. All-pervading, it is the nerve organism, the *esse* of things, the material out of which is developed our spiritual bodies.

Rev. Charles Beecher, as if to undermine the basis of Spiritualism, but thus virtually acknowledging it, says of this ethereal medium: "It was the Φύσις of Hippocrates, Aristotle, and Galen; the anima (as opposed to animus) of the Romans; and the Sephiroth of the Jewish Cabala. From this 'soul of the world' of the pre-Platonic Orientals, all souls are emanations. The 'demons' of the Greeks, from Plato down to Jamblichus, were nothing but this. By this the magicians of the Nile, and the jugglers of the Ganges, wrought their wonders. This was the true Python, source of all divination, magic, and witchcraft, in annals sacred and profane. This is the true secret of the Protean wonders of Rhabdomancy, clairvoyance, and animal magnetism."

"The occult science," says Father Rebold, "designated by the ancient priests under the name of regenerating fire, is that which at the present day is known as animal magnetism—a science that, for more than three thousand years, was the peculiar possession of the Indian and Egyptian priesthood, into the knowledge of which Moses was initiated at Heliopolis, when he was educated; and Jesus, among the Essenian priests of Egypt or Judea; and by which these two great reformers, particularly the latter, wrought many of the miracles mentioned in Scriptures."

Baron Reichenbach, detecting these elemental spheres around objects, which he termed " odylic," made many interesting experiments, indicating by what subtle influences we are all moved. Thus, seizing upon the very soul of this spiritual atmosphere, he was able to trace the photographing of mineral and metalic substances upon each other, of animals on animals, of man on man. He found that stars and clusters of stars have a magnetic influence peculiar to their aura.

SPHERES OF THINGS.

The experiments of many media have revealed a new magnetic science, of the greatest utility to the world. As every atom, every pebble, every mineral, every metal, every vegetable, every animal, is insphered with its own aura, there is here a talismanic line of invisible communication, detectable always by sensitive persons. Our clothes are pervaded with our spheres. Some one says that the sick consumptive weaves in the garment she makes a sickly element. Every one knows that food in some houses tastes better than in others— even if cooked by the same person. Why is food eaten out of doors, as in picnics, more palatable than even in palaces? Is it not because a freer, better magnetism has infused itself through it, out in the broad sunlight, under the electric trees?

Philosophers have been long puzzling their brains about the secret causes of civilization and national characteristics. Let them study the philosophy of spheres, and they will have positive data. Localities produce like characterestics on their inhabitants. There are places where no exalted spiritual community can possibly be generated or developed. Every village and city has its peculiar character, by virtue of the blended atmospheres of the natural and animal mag-netic forces locally exhaled there.

Certain stones and plants possess a peculiar mag-netic power of extracting diseases from the human body. Hidden springs of water and mines of oil, and minerals and metals, are detectable with certain persons of mediumistic powers. The animals and reptiles have a power of charming their prey. Man is generally the psychological master of the creation. All cower before him, when he understands and applies his art. Even the vegetable and mineral kingdoms assume new phases of being in his cultivated presence. All these strange possessions and transformations are due to the

electrical action of spheres acting on spheres, the
superior ever controlling.

HUMAN SPHERES.

Mr. Ruskin, writing to a friend in the North of
England, says: "You most probably have heard of
the marvelous power which chemical analysis has
received in recent discoveries respecting the laws of
light. My friend showed me the rainbow of the rose,
and the rainbow of the violet, and the rainbow of the
hyacinth, and the rainbow of the forest leaves being
born, and the rainbow of the forest leaves dying. And,
last, he showed me the rainbow of blood. It was but
the three-hundredth part of a grain, dissolved in a drop
of water; and it cast its measured bars, forever recognizable now to human sight, on the chord of the seven
colors. And no drop of that red rain can now be shed,
so small as that the stain of it cannot be known, and
the voice of it heard out of the ground."

The better to comprehend the source and nature of
our magnetic spheres, and their uses, we quote the following physiological and psychological analysis of the
human brain, with its nervous system: "The cerebral
ganglia," says a writer, "constitute the whole upper
and outer portion of the brain, found in all the higher
animals. They are composed of globulous matter,
from which innumerable fibres or threads extend
toward the centre of the brain. In this globulous
matter of the cerebrum all psycho-nervous action orig-
inates, and to it all communications are made that in

any way affect the psychical agent. It is this portion of the brain that constitutes nearly all the *organs* assigned to man in the science of Gall; and, according to Bællarger, its entire surface, when its convolutions are unfolded, is six hundred and seventy square inches. Moreover, the cerebral hemispheres of man include an amount of nervous matter which is four times that of all the rest of the cranio-spinal mass;—more than eight times that of the cerebellum, or little brain, thirteen times that of the medulla oblongata, and twenty-four times that of the spinal cord. And when the cerebrum of different animals is compared, it is found to be possessed in a superior degree by those animals most elevated in their physical developments. It is also found that for each additional convolution of the cerebrum some additional psychical function is found: thus showing that every particular centre of the cerebrum has a particular psychical function, whose law is to propagate its influence."

Dr. J. R. Buchanan, author of several anthropological works of value, says: "Man is becoming more and more a being of nerve and brain—the spiritual is advancing into a more complete domination of the material, and the region of conjunction between the material and spiritual, would naturally become the dominant region of the brain; and they who, as seers or clairvoyants, or mediums, are cultivating these higher faculties now, are directly aiding the progress of humanity in its higher evolution.

"Nature offers a coarser structure for coarser duties,

4

and a more refined one for subtler functions. The ganglion globules of the upper region of the brain are very different from the coarser and often multipolar structures of the base. The nerve fibre exhibits an ascending refinement of structure from that which performs the coarser muscular functions to that which has the more spiritual functions of the anterior lobe. Anatomists, without any pre-conceived theories, are struck with this fact, and find a difference of size, even as great in extremes as one to ten, between the highest cerebral fibres and those of the cerebro-spinal system, which are devoted to muscular motion."

MAGNETIC CURRENTS OF SPHERES.

By delicate experiments it is ascertained that our magnetic spheres have their currental and polar action analogous with the electrics circulating around the earth; operating by similar laws, susceptible to the control of more positive forces, and correlated with physico-mental batteries in every part of the universe, thus allying spirits in the flesh and out of the flesh in indissoluble bonds.

The ancient magicians called these currents, or "fluids," as some denominate it, "the living fire." Delaage, a French *Thaumaturge*, gives it the name of *l'esprit de vie*, and says " it has the color of fire on the electric spark, and is generative and plastic, inducing formation, and bending everything it touches into the forms prescribed by the directing intelligence. Soul of the world, spirit diffused through all nature, it is the vital essence of all the bodies which it animates, and of all the species in which it is incarnate; and is itself profoundly modified by all the mediums which it traverses. It is flesh when it traverses the flesh, and bone when it traverses the bones; and so truly is it the essence of each man, that if you present to a lucid somnambulist a lock of hair impregnated with this fluid, he will, in his super-normal condition, describe physically and morally the person from whose head it was taken."

The correctness of this statement of Delaage is illustrated in the grafting of scions that preserve their identical natures, though supplied with life-juices from the adopted tree of a different quality. So with skin-grafting, whereby a sore is healed, even though the healthy piece of skin may be taken from another person.

MAGNETIC PENETRABILITY.

The magnetic sphere, or the " psychic force," as the the English philosophers call it, which is employed by seen and unseen agency to convey intelligence, and by which spirits control their media, is, like electricity, all-pervading. Dr. William Gregory says: " We easily perceive that in highly susceptible cases, distance may be a matter of no moment; that our new force or influence may, like light, traverse the universe without difficulty, while, like heat, it may be able to penetrate through all objects, even through walls of brick or stone."

SPHERES OF SECTS.

A critical observer says of the " psychic force:" " As the human countenance photographs itself upon the sensitive silver plate, which it does not touch, so the human brain may odylise itself upon the sensitive cerebral plate of the medium which it does not touch. Or, as in every cranium two brains unite to form a double cerebral unit, so in space two brains filmily meshed together by odylic threads may virtually unite to form a double cerebral unit, the impressions of the stronger imparting themselves to and through the weaker. Thus things never known to the medium, apparently, or to any one in the circle, may be given forth by the distant automatic agency of some co-efficient brain."

All true, and by this law the sects are masked, as in " revivals." Thus, the " Holy Spirit," so-called, the church name for this " force," is formal and sedate with the Presbyterians, calm and rational with the Universalists, warm and passional with the Methodists and Mormons, sullenly devout with the Second Adventists, enliveningly varied with the Spiritualists, as are their conditions of mind and habits. With the " Jerkers," of Kentucky, it is convulsive; with the Shakers and Quakers it is spasmodic and inspirational. Its form is of the vessel through which it flows, tinging that vessel with its own spirit, just as the media are organized, educated and affectioned. This law is seen in the history of every nervous epidemic of past ages—in the Tarantalia of Italy, the St. John's dance of Germany, the St. Vitus' dance of France, the preaching mania of Sweden, the witch mania of Salem and Europe, the Flagellettes, or Penitents, or Holy Brotherhood, in Southern Colorado and New Mexico.

THE CHINESE REBELLION.

The Tai-ping rebellion, in China, was of a spiritual origin. Though reading of this in the New York journals, we could not get at the root of the matter until our (junior editor's) visit with Dr. Dunn to this ancient country. The daring movement originated with Hung-sew-tswen, born near Canton—a clairvoyant seer from infancy! When a lad, he was considered strange and eccentric. Returning to his home when a young man, from an unsuccessful examination, he was attacked with a severe sickness, during which he declared " that he had been favored with supernatural manifestations and revelations." He felt that "he had been washed from the impurities of his nature, and introduced into the presence of an august being, who exhorted him to live a virtuous life and exterminate demons." This "immortalized man, whom he often saw, of middle age, and dignified mien, further instructed him how to act." Hung called this visitant his "elder brother." About this time he read the New Testament and declared immediately thereafter " that this imposing personage seen in his visions was Jesus Christ, the sent-of-God." A scholarly friend of his, named Le, uniting with him, they commenced preaching, baptising, and making converts. During their inflammatory discourses, persons would fall into the trance, speak in strange tongues, and utter alleged revelations and prophesies. They organized to protect themselves and punish their persecutors. This led to war; the insurrection became formidable, and for a time successful. Multitudes perished by sword and famine; vacated fields and burned cities yet in ruins, remain to tell the tale of war. The purpose was to overthrow the reigning dynasty and destroy the idols of the land.

Hung-sew-tswen, now putting himself at the head of the new Kingdom, was styled *Tai-ping tien Kwoh*, assuming the title "Son of Heaven." He professed to have direct communications from God, and spoke very familiarly of Jesus as his brother. He continually read the Old Testament, and observed religious worship in his camp. He assured missionaries that his revelations were as authoritative as those of the Bible, and he could prove it by his divine gifts. Loyal Chinamen call him and his soldiers "long-haired rebels." Successes corrupting his leading officers with envies and jealousies in different camps, the Emperor's armies, aided by General Ward and the English, the Tai-ping rebellion was put down. The struggle continued fourteen years. The leading spirit of the rebellious host committed suicide. Those caught by the government officials were tortured and massacred. Hung-sew-tswen's teachings continued to produce their results. His admirers believed him to have been God-inspired for a purpose, as was Moses, of Hebrew memory.

CONTAGIOUS MADNESS.

The terrible scenes which accompanied the final sup-
pression of the French Commune, in 1870, is attributed
to a "contagious mental alienation." It was verily a
magnetic madness — a national tempest arising from
starvation and epidemical passion. "The minds of the
Parisians were gradually unhinged by the privations of
the siege. The revolt of the eighteenth of March gave
the last blow to brains which were already shaken, and
at length the greater part of the population went raving
mad. The records of the Middle Ages are full of similar
examples. * * * Women are, under such circumstances, fiercer and more reckless than men. This is
because their nervous system is more developed, their
brains are weaker, and their sensibilities more acute
than those of the stronger sex; and they are consequently far more dangerous, and do much more harm.
* * * None of them knew exactly what they were
fighting for; they were possessed by one of the various
forms of the religious mania—that which impelled the
Jansenists to torture themselves, with a strange delight
in pain of the acutest kind. * * * The men who
threw themselves on the bayonets of the soldiers in a
paroxysm of passion, were seen ten minutes after
utterly prostrate and begging for mercy. They were
no more cowards in the last state than they were heroes
in the first—they were simply madmen."

Such facts should warn us to look into the cause of
national madness. The toiling millions, as with the

French Communes, who struck for democratic liberty, cannot long endure the burdens laid upon their shoulders by tyrants. It needs no prophet's eye to see that our own America is fast moving into one of these magnetic maelstroms! If we would avert a Parisian Reign of Terror, instruct the masses in their rights, secure them their rights, enlighten them in these spiritual laws and social relations.

VACCINATION.

We little know how subtlely and stealthily the fine and invisible elements or virus of pestilences and diseases of varied kinds, fall upon and impregnate our very vitals, when we touch them in negative conditions of mind and body, induced by fear or neglect. Vaccination, for instance, meant for a benevolent purpose, made popular by long use, as a preventive against the small-pox, has proved by experiment to be a source of incalculable mischief. Every element introduced into the human system not only taints it with its own nature, but is tainted in turn with the nature of the system itself. The cow-pox virus changes the quality of the blood, and the blood in turn its quality. Matter from persons' arms who are afflicted with consumption or scrofula, or syphilitic diseases, will, of course, engender like diseases and conditions even in the most healthful organism. The havoc thus made is fearful. Vaccination not only transmits diseases and insanities, but moral conditions. A particle of such virus from a vicious person whose habits are low and groveling,

may induce the worst phases of carnal infestation!
"Mr. William Field, of Oxford street, England, President of the Veterinary College, says grease in the horse is always accompanied by diseased lungs. W. C. Collins, Esq., M. D., says two hundred and fifty thousand deaths annually occur from consumption, pneumonia convulsions, atrophy, and other strumous diseases, occasioned or superadded by vaccination. Consumption, scrofula, and other blood diseases, were comparatively unknown before the introduction of inoculation and cow-pox vaccination. 'It is our duty,' said the report of the first Vaccine Institution, 'to acknowledge that four or five cases have proved fatal from the effects of vaccination.'

"Dr. Bayard, a French physician of eminence, in a petition which he sent to the British House of Commons, by Mr. Ayrton, of the Tower Hamlets, said: 'Since vaccination, the mortality of the young has doubled; and, contemporaneously with the increase of mortality, we have a diminution of births, an increase of the general death rates, and the number of second marriages.'

"Dr. Copland, in his *Medical Dictionary*, page 829, says: 'Just half a century has elapsed since the discovery and introduction of vaccination, and after a quarter of a century of transcendental laudation of the measure, from well-paid vaccination boards, raised with a view of overbearing the increasing murmurings of disbelief in all those who observe and think for themselves, the middle of the nineteenth century finds

5

the majority of the profession in all latitudes—doubtful of its advantages, either from inoculation or vaccination.'"

MAGNETIC DEFILEMENT.

It is a law of "second sight," that whoever touches a seer during a vision, is enabled, if impressible, to see the same. Sensitive persons, by touching Mrs. Hauffe, when she had visions of spectres, were made to see them also. Our magnetism is virtually our self-hood refined into spirit essence, what we are in qualities of mental and physical composition, sphered around in aural light. Being derived from all we are and all we appropriate to use, whatever food we eat, or fluid we drink, or clothing we wear, or emotion cherish, or habit engender, or thought produce, deposits in this sphere its own qualitative essence compounded together for crystallization or structure, and thence insphered in corresponding magnetism. As the most minute grain of musk will scent a room even for centuries, so does the least element of our magnetism reflect exactly what we are in quality of mind and body.

As magnetic spheres are communicable, suffusing whatever they affinitively touch, we do not wonder the ancient Hebrews, understanding these facts, instituted severe laws against magnetic defilement. There is wisdom in the Levitical laws (Leviticus xxii.) which we shall do well to study:

"Say unto them, Whosoever *he be* of all your seed, among your generations, that goeth unto the holy things, which the children of Israel hallow unto the Lord, having his uncleanness upon him, that soul shall be cut off from my presence: I *am* the Lord. What man soever of the seed of Aaron *is* a leper, or hath a running issue, he shall not eat of the holy things, until he be clean. And whoso toucheth any thing *that is* unclean *by* the dead, or a man whose seed goeth from him; Or whosoever toucheth any creeping thing, whereby he may be made unclean, or a man of whom he may take uncleanness, whatsoever uncleanness he hath; The soul which hath touched any such shall be unclean until even, and shall not eat of the holy things, unless he wash his flesh with water."

POWER OF MAGNETIC SPHERES.

They are the secret force of battle, and of all action. A single fact will illustrate it in domestic life: " A curious case of mesmerism is recorded by the civil surgeon of Hoshungabad, India. A young woman named Nunnee, aged twenty-four, married some twelve years ago. She, however, did not go to her husband's house for two years afterward. After staying with him for eight years, she suddenly became insensible, and remained so for two or three days. She was taken back to her mother, and soon got well. Then follows a very remarkable history. During the next four or five years she never entered her husband's house without falling insensible and remaining so. He was very kind and attentive to her; she liked him, but whenever he came into her presence she at once sank into this state. This went on till she became emaciated and exhausted, and at last her parents applied to the court for a separate maintenance for her. While she was in court the husband entered, and she instantly became insensible, and was carried to the hospital, where the case was carefully attended to by Dr. Cullen, in March, this year. While in this state her pulse was even, breathing soft, her body pliant, but she could eat nothing. Experiments were carefully made to see if there was no trick about it. While she was in bed, her husband was muffled up, and made to walk through the ward. She said she felt he was near her, and she was by no means well, but had not seen him anywhere about. Next day this experiment was repeated, and she actually became insensible as before. When the husband left the place she recovered. The experiment as to the influence of the husband's presence was tried in all sorts of ways. He was made to pass behind her, and be near her in a separate ward, but this had no effect; but whenever he was brought to look on her face, though muffled up, or disguised as a policeman, as a Sepoy, etc., she was at once influenced. The experiments continued for about a month, and the conclusion was that the husband unconsciously mesmerized her. The court came to the conclusion that it was impossible that she could live with him, and a separate allowance was ordered. The husband was asked to try if he could not remove the effect, seeing that he had the power to cause it, but he was quite frightened at the idea of having the power, and could not control it in any way."

The query often is mooted why the American Indians recede and die off so rapidly before the whites. It is not so much the conquest of the sword as the magnetic disparity between the two races. The magnetism of the whites is death to the Indians—poisons them, literally sucks out all their life forces. Wild by nature, they extract the wild from forests, waterfall and battle, and then—if unmolested—are healthful and happy, virtuous and spiritual.

David G. Briton, in his "Myths of the New World," speaking of the Indians, says: "In these strange duels à l'outrance, one would be seated opposite his antagonist, surrounded with the mysterious emblems of his craft, and call upon his gods, one after another, to strike his enemy dead. Sometimes one, gathering his medicine, as it was termed, feeling within himself that hidden force of will which makes itself acknowledged even without words, would rise in his might, and in a loud and severe voice command his opponent to die! Straightway the latter would drop dead, or, yielding in craven fear to a superior volition, forsake the implements of his art, and, with an awful terror at his heart, creep to his lodge, refuse all nourishment, and presently perish. Still more terrible was the tyranny they exerted on the superstitious mind of the masses. Let an Indian once be possessed of the idea that he is bewitched, and he

will probably reject all food, and sink under the
phantoms of his own fancy."

IGNORANT INJURIES.

Every one who has thought knows that children
sleeping with old people lose their vitality and droop
often into premature death, while the aged thus pro-
long their lives. This is a wrong. Children need all
their magnetism and all they can glean, to grow and
take the place of the declining generations, who should
be glad to go when fully ripe. There are magnetic
relations here little understood, but by no means " the
Mysteries of Providence," no more than any other
sequence of cause. We know of frequent instances
where departed mothers have, from sympathy, drawn
their children to them—actually slew them by magnetism, sometimes to avert a prophetic calamity, and as
often unconscious in their loving ignorance—though
spirits—of the death they produce till they are received
into their bosoms. We know of cases where men have
killed their wives, and wives their husbands, by a slow
magnetic depletion, and where spirits, too, from pur-
posed design, benevolent or malicious, have educed
calamities, sickness and death.

REVIVALS.

It is well known that the prayer of a powerful revi-
valist will affect a negative congregation, frightening
men, women and children into an insane frenzy; and
that it will magnetize even a negative person not pres-

ent, when all the wills are centered to convert him. Under diabolical purposes and infestations, we know of parties, in a so-called spiritual circle, who have sought to kill another psychologically, and would have succeeded but for the timely interference of a guardian angel, who reported the plot. We would warn the unwary, and enjoin careful inspection and moral courage, lest the "lively oracles" may prove their snare.

HEALING SPHERES.

It is an admitted fact that there are sixty-four substances, known as primaries, entering into the composition of all things in Nature. In the original rocks they exist in original fibre; in the soils formed by deposition they are finer; in plants and animals, most fine and active, they seem to lie beyond the reach of chemical analysis. As Nature progresses in her serial orders, they become more and more potential. Nature's laboratory creates differences which escape the chemist.

When a primary, originally from the rock, thence from the soil, thence from the plant, enters the animal, it has progressed beyond any known chemical recognition; but it is then in full lordship. When, by decay of the plant and animal, the primary returns to the soil, it is capable of being absorbed by an improved plant and animal. By these changes the lichens and mosses, the first forms of vegetation, are fitted for higher assimilations and the growth of more refined and beautiful organisms.

A double rose cannot be sustained in the fresh *debris*

of rock from the mountain; but a single rose growing there, transplanted to the older soil of the garden, will gradually become double. The reason is, the primaries have here been in transitional organic life many times, furnishing the right elemental nutrition for the new-comer. Thus Nature absolutely refuses to retrograde; her decays are sources of progression.

Sulphate of lime, made from bones, is worth to the farmer a great per cent. more than its own weight of sulphate of lime from the native plaster of Paris. When direct from the rock it is almost inefficient. It must first pass through the chain of progression, reaching the highest forms of organic life, ere it is fitted for the improved agricultural purposes.

Apple trees will not grow and thrive in certain parts of the Northwest, especially in the border regions of civilization, not on account of climate, but from want of progression in the primaries forming the necessary pabulum.

It is well known that the more refined and medical properties are, the more potent they are. No blending of ingredients, though the same in kind, will produce effects like the waters of the mineral spring. Art fails in that it cannot make the soul of things. Well-read physicians of the different schools tell us that the most powerful medicines, prussic acid, for instance, are extracted from the vegetable kingdom. Why superior to those from the mineral? Because Nature has progressed one step. Could chemistry extract the medical properties existing in the organs of animals, we would have an approximate spiritual system of cure. Iron from blood must surely be more efficacious than iron from the mine held in similar solution. It has been proved that medicine from the calcined bones of animals possesses altogether a more potential virtue than that from the calcined phosphates of lime rock. Chemically they are the same, but spiritually they are different. The reason is that the primaries in the bones are progressions from the rock. What now of magnetism? Its every particle involves the nature of the individual whence it is produced. Sublimated element, the very essence of all organic forms and vitalities in creation, the attenuation of all refinements, the spirit's atmosphere charged with all medical properties progressed from every order of form and being up to man, the super-angel of the material universe, it contains the primaries in their perfection, and, according to what is revealed in the lower strata of life, already traced, whereby we see unity of force everywhere, it is the only thorough and searching remedy that can be applied to our physically and mentally diseased humanity. It moves and controls human tides as sent forth from positive wills. It is a power, when lovingly used, that shall lift the nations to God. If it is spiritualized by coming into *rapport* with the electrifying batteries of spirit-hands, spirit-hearts and spirit-brains, as is the case with a well-disciplined healing medium, it is the conqueror of disease, death, and hell itself.

" Mrs. Cora L. V. Tappan, on the twenty-seventh

of March, 1870, replied, under spirit control, to the inquiry, 'Who should be healers?' substantially as follows: 'All are healers, slayers, or both. * * * Every one you meet is benefited or injured by your magnetism. Medicines differently affect, according to those by whom they are administered. The great study of healers should be to endeavor to cure only those to whom they are medicinal.' "

SOUND OF SPHERES.

As all things emit magnetic spheres producing sensations, is it not inferential that they move in undulations, like light? And as they impinge against resisting media, doubtless they are accompanied with sounds. "The 'Medical Times,' " says the 'Boston Transcript,' " translates from a German medical journal an account of the first case known of persons receiving visual impressions from sound, in the instance of two brothers named Nussbaumer, who, when a certain note on the piano is struck, have a sensation of a certain corresponding color, which is not, however, identical for both. For illustration, the note which produces in one the impression of dark Prussian blue, produces the sensation of a dark yellow in the other. One of them, according to the account, has frequent sensations of yellow, brown and violet; while blue, yellow and brown are frequent with the other. One of them never receives the sensation of red, green, black or white, in connection with musical notes, though the filing of a saw may produce a sensation of green. Professor Brühl, of Vienna, has thoroughly tested this strange case, and has no doubt of the genuineness of the phenomena."

" This effect of musical tones," adds David Wilder, in the ' Banner of Light,' " was observed in this city as early as the year 1861, and as the lady who possessed the peculiar power is still living here, I have no doubt that the experiment then tried might be repeated with success.

" Another lady (the authoress of ' Dawn '), at about the same time, said she was able to hear sounds, when standing before paintings, and it would seem that there might also be a third sense opened, and musical tones be found to have not only color, but odor."

" We can endorse the remarks of the writer," says the editor of the " Banner," " to the full; Mrs. Conant was the first lady referred to, and in our presence she has, in a clairvoyant state, frequently described the differing colors perceived by her when listening to distinct musical sounds."

How discordant, therefore, are the oscillating forces of a malignant sphere! how easily detected! how are we repelled from such jars! It is the unutterable groanings from the soul's hells of perversity. How sweet and musical the presence of orderly spheres, attuned to aspiration after goodness! A holy angel trails music all along the shining way.

Swedenborg discovered the practicability of this musical ratiocination in the spiritual world, when he said, all the speech of angels, " at the close of every sentence, has its termination in unity of accent, which is merely in consequence of the divine influx into their souls respecting the unity of God."

ODOR OF SPHERES.

The human soul, like the life of everything that is sentient, has a species of its own, evolving an odorous atmosphere exactly in ratio with its inner affections. The experience of every medium substantiates this. Undoubtedly whatever we take into our bodies gives a shade or odor corresponding with the nature of the element. But the *data* of such " smell " is in the spiritual organism. Whenever the affection and ruling habit of this is changed, a like change occurs with the temperamental odors of our spheres. The Seer of Sweden, sensing these variable odors, informs us that the " effluvia " from unregenerate spirits is nauseating to the interiorly unfolded. He says: " Evil and good cannot abide together, and in proportion as evil is removed good is regarded and felt, because in the spiritual world there exhales from every one the sphere of his particular love, which diffuses itself and gives forth its influences all around, causing sympathies and antipathies; by means of such spheres the good are separated from the evil."

COLOR OF SPHERES.

As each mental impulse moves the machinery of the body, so in turn this machinery of organs and functions, as the mind's medium refined into sphere, undulates outward like sunbeams, in vibratory action, ever voicing the intensity and atomic force of such impulse, producing corresponding colors, by similar laws governing light. Every color in the sphere reports the mental and moral status of the individual. Spirits and mortals are therefore seen in diversely colored habiliments. With persons of inverted loves, where the habits are gross and animal, such appear more or less darkened and hazy. The sphere or clothing of a dark spirit is murky. Around the merely intellectual it appears clear, cold and positive, with bluish shadings. Around the genial, spiritual and harmonial, it is bright and silvery, mellowing into the golden. This idea is elaborated in the Scriptures with reference to spirit-clothing. Matthew writes: "The angel of the Lord descended from heaven, rolled back the stone from the door, * * * and his raiment was *white as snow*." Luke says, "They found the stone rolled away, * * * and two men stood by them in *shining garments*." It is said that on the mount, "Jesus' face did shine as the sun, * * * and his raiment was white as the light." When Cornelius was praying, "A man stood before him in bright clothing." The light that shone around about Paul was "above the brightness of the sun;" and John, entranced upon the Isle of Patmos, perceived that those who had "*overcome were clothed in white robes*."

During one of our (senior editor's) night entrancements, we saw in lucid vision a most magnificent combination of music, odor and color, all proceeding from celestial light; saw spirits, and heard their voices. The time will come when earth's inhabitants will make such privileges their highest aspiration.

CHAPTER IV.

OBSESSION is from the Latin *obsessio*—besieging; the state of a person vexed or besieged by evil spirits— *i. e.*, lower orders of spiritual beings.

Necromancy is from the Greek, *nekros*, a corpse, and *manteia*, divination, implying the method of foreknowing future events by calling upon the dead and questioning them.

Devil and demon should never be confounded. They are not interchangeable terms.

The Greek term for devil is *diabolus*, and signifies slanderer, traducer, spy. The orthodox Dr. Campbell says: "The word *diabolus*, in its ordinary acceptation, signifies calumniator, traducer, false accuser, from the verb *diaballein*, to calumniate. Hence we read in 1 Timothy, iii: 11, 'Even so must their wives be grave, not slanderers (*diabolus*), sober, faithful in all things.' Here, the pious women of the early Christian Churches are exhorted not to be slanderers— literally, 'not to be devils.' Jesus says, John vi: 70, "Have not I chosen you twelve? and one of you (Judas) is a devil."

The word *Satan*, theologically made to signify a demi-god of evil, an individual "*prince of darkness*," is the Hebrew common noun signifying an adversary, an enemy, an opposition, etc., and is used in that sense in the Bible. Thus in 1 Kings xi: 14, Hadad, as an adversary of Solomon, is called *Satan* in the original text. Also in the same chapter, twenty-third verse, Rezon, an adversary, is denominated *Satan*. David was called *Satan* in the twenty-ninth chapter of Samuel: and the angel of the Lord, which appeared unto Balaam, or rather unto his ass first, was denominated *Satan*, etc.

The Vedas, Puranas and Upanishads, abound in references to the *Devatas* and *Soors*—good angels and subordinate celestial beings—and to the *Dews, Asoors* and *Danoos*—evil spirits, and the method of destroying their influences. Upham says this "doctrine of demons, in full force to-day in the island of Ceylon, is older than Buddhism. Gotama found it when he there made his appearance, in the year 540 B. C." (Ast. Res. viii: 531).

In a moral and social sense, obsession is a magnetic monopoly that brings us into unnatural relations, educing physical and spiritual discords and diseases. Wherever is an obtrusion upon the laws of order, whether by force or stealth, unbalance follows; and when this obtrusion proceeds from the will of a mortal or spirit for a selfish end, holding by magnetic action, it is obsession.

Jamblichus, closely observing the phenomena of obsession, exactly corroborates modern experience:

"But, in truth, inspiration is the work neither of

soul nor body, nor of their entire compound. The true cause is no other than illumination emanating from the very gods themselves, and spirits coming forth from them, and an obsession by which they hold us fully and absolutely, absorbing all our faculties even, and exterminating all human motions and operations, even to consciousness itself; bringing discourses which they who utter them do not understand, but pronounce with furious lip, so that our whole being becomes secondary and subservient to the sole power of the occupying god."

Hermes says "when a demon flows into a human soul he sprinkles in it seeds of his own notions, whence such a soul sprinkled with seeds, raised in a fury, brings forth wonderful things."

Zoroaster taught that the devs or evil spirits "entered the bodies of men and produced all manner of diseases. They entered their minds and incited them to sensuality, falsehood, slander and revenge."

Proclus, of the Alexandrian philosophy, and teacher of Athens, classified the spirits in different orders— "the highest as uniform and divine."

Porphyry, a Phœnician of the third century, and a professor of the Alexandrian School, spoke often of "the power of evil spirits" as causes of "personal quarrels and national wars," and affirmed that evil demons "inflamed women, corrupted boys, and spread terrors among those who did not examine things by reason." Not realizing they were a lower order of spirits, "they called them gods, and gave to each the

name he claimed for himself; but Socrates endeavored
to expose their practices, and by true reason draw men
away from their influences, and the demons, by the
help of wicked men, caused this Grecian philosopher
to be put to death as an atheist and impious person."
According to certain phenomena of the present, does
not this statement concerning Socrates bear the
semblance of truth?

JEWISH OBSESSIONS.

Renan, in his "Life of Jesus," himself a scholastic
materialist, attempting to explain all psychic phenomena by the known laws of physical science, and signally
failing, as all such do and must—for how can the physical correlate the spiritual in full measure, or the
material eye see principles?—gives credence to the
prevailing beliefs in obsessions, even with the best
of scholars: "A singular readiness to believe in
demons reigned in all minds. It was a universal opinion, not only in Judea, but in the whole world, that
demons take possession of certain persons and make
them act contrary to their own will. The Persian
div named many times in the Avesta *Aeschma*,
daeva, the '*div* of concupiscence,' adopted by the
Jews under the name of Asmodeus, became the cause
of all hysterical troubles among women. * * *
The vocation of an exorcist was a regular profession
like that of the physician. * * * Almost down
to our day the men who have done most for the good
of their kind (the excellent Vincent de Paul himself!)

6

have been, whether they wished it or not, Thaumatur-
gists. The School of Alexandria was a noble school,
and yet it abandoned itself to the practice of an
extravagant thaumaturgy."

According to the record some of the ancient Hebrew
prophets were guilty of habitual obsessions; so also
were certain early Christians accused of " fornication:"
" Wherefore their way shall be unto them as slippery
ways in the darkness; they shall be driven on, and fall
therein: for I will bring evil upon them, even the year
of their visitation, saith the Lord. And I have seen
folly in the prophets of Samaria; they prophesied in
Baal, and caused my people Israel to err. I have seen
also in the prophets of Jerusalem a horrible thing; they
commit adultery, and walk in lies; they strengthen
also the hands of evil-doers, that none doth return
from his wickedness; they are all of them unto me as
Sodom, and the inhabitants thereof as Gomorrah.
Therefore thus saith the Lord of hosts concerning the
prophets, Behold, I will feed them with wormwood,
and make them drink the water of gall, for from the
prophets of Jerusalem is profaneness gone forth into
all the land."—Jeremiah xxiii: 11–15.

MODERN REFERENCES.

Wolfgang Muscalus, Professor of Divinity at Berne,
a disciple of Luther, speaking of demons, says: " These
malignant spirits lurk in statues and images, inspire
soothsayers, compose oracles, influence the flight of
birds, trouble life, disquiet sleep, distort the members,
break down the health and harass with diseases."

The poet Milton thus refers to the subtilties of demons:

> " But when lust,
> By unchaste looks, loose gestures, and foul talk,
> But most by lewd and lavish act of sin,
> Lets in defilement to the inward parts,
> That soul grows clotted by contagion;
> Imbodies and imbrutes till she quite lose
> The divine property of her first being.
> Such are those thick and gloomy shadows damp,
> Or seen in charnal vaults and sepulchers;
> Lingering and sitting by a new-made grave;
> As loth to leave the body that it loved,
> And linked itself by carnal sensuality
> To a degenerate and degraded state."

"Wesley believed that devils (demons) produced disease and bodily hurts; that epilepsy and insanity often proceeded from demon influence. He declared that if he gave up faith in witchcraft, he must give up the Bible. When asked whether he had himself seen a ghost, he replied, 'No; nor have I ever seen a murder; but unfortunately I am compelled to believe that murders take place almost every day, in one place or another.' Warburton attacked Wesley's belief in miraculous cures and expulsion of evil spirits; but Wesley replied that what he had seen with his own eyes, he was bound to believe; the Bishop could believe or not, as he pleased."

HOW SPIRITS TORMENTED SWEDENBORG.

The following are extracts from Swedenborg's Spiritual Diary:

"September, 1747.—From experience I have learned that evil spirits cannot desist from tormenting. By their presence they have inflicted pains upon different parts of my body, as upon my feet, so that I could scarcely walk; upon the dorsal nerves, so that I could scarcely stand, and upon parts of my head with such pertinacity that the pains lasted for some hours. I was clearly instructed that such sufferings are inflicted upon men by evil spirits.

"October 21, 1748.—Evil spirits throw in troublesome, inconvenient and unhappy suggestions, and aggravate and confirm my anxiety. Hence arise the melancholy of many people, debilitated minds, deliriums, insanities, phantasies.

"January 8, 1748.—When I was about to go to sleep, it was stated that certain spirits were conspiring to kill me, but because I was secure I feared nothing, and fell asleep. About the middle of the night I awoke, and felt that I did not breathe from myself, but, as I believe, from heaven. It was then plainly told me that whole hosts of spirits had conspired to suffocate me, and as soon as they made the attempt, a heavenly respiration was opened in me and they were defeated."

[The heavenly respiration to which Swedenborg refers, or an interior magnetic breathing, is a frequent experience among well-disciplined media of to-day. It is indeed a "heavenly respiration," and a saving life to body and spirit. Only as one becomes spiritual and associated with the angels of wisdom can this divine principle be actualized. By such breathing the plane of our spiritual status can be determined.]

"January 11, 1748.—I observed that certain spirits often wished to excite me to steal things of small value, such as are met with in shops, and so great was their desire that they actually moved my hand.

"February 6.—I ascertained that in the world these spirits had been trades-people, who, by various artifices, defrauded their customers, and thought it allowable. Some had been celebrated merchants, at which I wondered. They wander about searching for things to steal, and whenever detected are punished with stripes and blows. When they were with me, as soon as I saw anything in shops, or any pieces of money, or the like, their cupidity became manifest to me; for thinking themselves to be me, they urged that I should stretch forth my hand to steal, quite contrary to my usual state and custom.

"There was a certain woman (Sara Hesselia) who inwardly cherished such an aversion to her parents that she meditated poisoning them. She took it into her head that I was willing to marry her, and when she found out that she was mistaken, she was seized with such a hatred that she thought of killing me, had it been possible. She died not long afterward. Some time before the faculty of conversing with spirits was opened in me, I was impelled to commit suicide with a knife. The impulse grew so strong that I was forced to hide the knife out of my sight in my desk. I have now discovered that Sara Hesselia was the spirit who excited the suicidal impulse as often as I saw the knife. From this it may appear that men may be unconsciously infested with spirits who hated them during their life on earth."

CASE OF RELIGIOUS OBSESSION.

Jung Stilling, in his Pneumatology, cites thus to a case of sensuous obsession, often paralleled these days: " A pious young woman visited the religious meetings which a pious, but handsome and married man, held in his house. By degrees she fell in love with him; and as insuperable difficulties stood in the way of her attachment, her nerves at length succumbed in the conflict, and the poor unfortunate girl became a somnambulist. At the commencement she uttered the most sublime and glorious truths in her fits; and she generally entered the crisis when present at these religious meetings. She predicted many things that were to happen in the future, several of which were accomplished. She gained a number of followers; and the most sensible and well-informed regarded her as one that was inspired by the Spirit of God—in a word, as a prophetess.

" In her fits she received information by degrees that the wife of the object of her affection was an abomination in the sight of God and his angels. This was gradually insinuated with such satanic cunning and hypocrisy that the whole company, which consisted of several hundred persons, most devoutly believed it. The poor woman was, therefore, confined in a remote place, by orders from the invisible world. She lost her reason, and died raving mad; and the widower then married the young woman, also by an order from the spirits."

THE MORZINE OBSESSIONS.

Speaking of the obsessions at Morzine, Dr. Arthan, a governmental agent of France, says: "Healthy and pious mothers, some with child, some nursing, uttered blasphemies and used language which the most degraded would stare at. Respectable girls blasphemed all they believed most sacred. Children grew strangely and irrepressibly insolent. A general moral disorganization has changed all the habits of the village. Why has this happened at Morzine? The people of the neighboring parish are entirely exempt, though its chaplets are within a stone's throw of houses that have been visited by this spiritual plague. * * *

"I observed in every case more or less marked:

"The abnormal development of muscular force.

"The intellectual excitement producing marvelous lucidity of thought, and correctness of language.

"Cries, blasphemies and imprecations.

"The personation of the evil spirits by the patients, who spoke of themselves in the third person always."

UNHAPPY SPIRITS.

Emma Hardinge refers, in the following, to Francis Smith, of Baltimore, now summering in the spirit world. It is parallel with the experience of thousands: "A similar case to the above occurs in the history of

one of the most pure, estimable and intelligent gentle-
men whom I have had the good fortune to meet in the
ranks of American Spiritualists. I speak of the accomplished author of a little book entitled 'Footsteps of a
Presbyterian.' This gentleman recently informed me
that his long and highly-prized intercourse with the
spirit world had been interrupted for a period of several years by the continued infestation of a dark,
ignorant and malignant spirit, whose presence has
driven away all other spirits, and forced him, by his
incessant and detestable influence, to abandon any
effort to communicate with spirits through his own
mediumistic organization. Before this terrible haunter
had entirely possessed himself of his victim, he induced
him to transcribe a narrative of his earth-life and spiritual experiencies; and these appeared to me so full
of instruction and suggestion that I induced my friend,
after narrating them to me, to put them in print, which
he has accordingly done in a little pamphlet just
published, entitled 'Life in the Beyond.' "

William Howitt, of England, the Christian Spiritualist, citing to numerous facts in proof of his
statement, demonstrates that obsessions largely prevail among so-called Christians, and that the popular
doctrine of the church, used as an excuse, has an inevitable bias to such infestation. After speaking of the
elevating influence which results from the communications of the good and holy spirits, and the exalting
effects which their ministrations produce on their
media, he goes on to say:

" Far different is the condition of others. They desire good equally and earnestly; they pray fervently and continuously for it; but evil is with them. With them the approach of spirits is not a visit, nor simply a visitation, but an inroad. They come, the door once open, in crowds, in mobs, in riotous invasions. They run, they leap, they fly, they gesticulate, they sing, they whoop, and they curse. They are the most merry and the most bitter of mockers. Wit looms in their words, like flashes of infernal lightning; pantomime is in their action; laughter in their eyes; and a horror which no assumption of innocence can veil, is the effluvia of their presence. There is no question with the wretched sufferers of their phantasmagorial assaults that they are the life and quintessence of hell. Nor is it the mind only of the unfortunate one which they haunt; they have a power over his material movements. They move and remove articles; they fling and toss; they hide and steal; they put things where they ought not to be; they take them from whence they should constantly be. Mind, body, soul, memory and imagination—nay, the very heart—are polluted by the ghostly *canaille;* and the sanctuary of life and the dwelling are invaded, disordered, desecrated, and made miserable by them. We have known such sufferers, and know them still. When they have written, praying for advice, how to get rid of this pestilence, we could only say, ' Pray with all your might for it; and stick close to the Savior who cast out these tormentors

7

in his earth-life. Pray without ceasing; pray in the might and faith of Christ.'

"It has been in vain! No prayer, no agony of petition, no persistence of a holy and wrestling exorcism has been able to dislodge the foul and murderous crew. There they were, and there they are!

"But we have not reached the abysmal depth of the dark mysteries of the spirit world. There is a fact more startling still, if these spirit prowlers on the border lands of life are to be credited on their own assurances. When asked, and that by different persons in different places, 'Why do you intrude on me, and persist in your intrusion, though commanded to depart?' the answer has been 'Because we live on you. Through your atmosphere we enter into the atmosphere of human life. That is our happiness; we know none else. We have none here; here all is dark, barren and joyless. We long to be back again in the warm, bright life of the earth; and we achieve it through you. You are our highway, our bridge, our door, along which we travel, over which we pass, and through which we enter, and again possess the heritage we had lost. In your emanations we revel; through your nostrils we once more snuff up the aromas of the earth, the scent of the feast and the wine cup; through your eyes open upon us, as of old, all the sweet varieties of life.'

"Struck with horror, one of these persecuted sufferers exclaimed: 'But this is a species of spiritual vampirism!'

" ' How so?' asked one of the tormentors. ' Every grade of animal life lives upon another. For your physical sustenance you live on the animal tribes; for your spiritual sustenance you live on Christ. He gives himself for the food of mankind. By his flesh and blood you exist. He is that living bread which came down from heaven, and we live on you and through you.' " * * *

Commenting on these statements of Mr. Howitt, Emma Hardinge adds, in respect to the trial made to cast out such spirits in the " name, faith and might of Christ," which signally failed:

" What a comment, too, on the doctrine of vicarious atonement and ' salvation through the blood of Christ' is the existence of these legions of undeveloped spirits at all! All of them are human spirits—nine-tenths of them once belonged to the ranks of Christianity; all of them lived beneath its shadow and teachings on earth. If Christ came on earth and died to save sinners, how is it that we hear of such terrible swarms of the unsaved? The good do not need saving; the bad are evidently not saved. If these tremendous revelations from the lost souls—the very class for whom we are to suppose the wonderful scheme of Christian salvation was invented—persist in returning to prove the fallacy and failure of that scheme, and even as good Mr. Howitt's communication implies, use that scheme as an argument why they should prey upon those who, in turn, prey upon the body and blood of Christ, must we not look soon for a new and more

effective scheme of salvation than the old ? — one
that will, as good old Pompey says, 'save sinners as
are sinners, not saints as is a shamming by cry-
ing, 'Lord, have mercy upon us miserable sinners!' Certain it is, despite all the power, splendor
and wealth with which blind devotion has upheld for
centuries the enormous ecclesiastical hierarchies of
christendom, the revelations of modern Spiritualism
prove with tremendous force that the good and the bad
are alike in the exact compensation and retribution of
their earthly acts and deeds, and that neither the name
nor the blood of Christ have power to control demons,
or in any way affect the condition of the human soul
here or hereafter."

According to the following statement of William
Howitt, literary persons, as well as illiterate, fall a prey
to these magnetic insanities:

" Bunyan, whose life at times they made a terror of
darkness and blasphemy, paid no court or homage to
them, but to very different powers. Cowper, whose
poetry is especially conspicuous for its sober and sound
sense, coquetted with no pseudo nymphs from Orcus,
but was driven by them through the deepest caverns
of despair, and to the very verge, time upon time, of
suicide. By a recent Memoir of the Abbé Lamennais,
we find that was exactly his condition also. The soul
murderers were upon him with all their inferal power.
They murdered his peace as completely as if he had
been the most desperate of criminals; and that noble
spirit which preached the religion of purity and love

in its divinest truth and beauty, was a prey to the
most agonizing despairs."

We know of persons, who, fearful of contamination and habitually animal, invite what they profess
to hate. When an evil spirit comes they are mad,
and vociferate, "Go away, G—d d—n ye!" As if
such a will could drive away! The very condition
holds the obsessing influence. None fall so easy a
prey as the mediumistic. The almost savage demands
for tests psychologically evoke a disposition to over-
rate. The electric conditions, thus engendered, defeat
the object. Hence the "despairs."

The agency of evil as well as good spirits is almost
universally conceded by the Spiritual speakers, writers
and media of to-day. Among them are Allen Putnam, Sam'l Watson, A. E. Giles, S. B. Brittan, W. D.
Gunning, and other prominent lights both in America
and Europe.

"They will deceive us for our amusement."—H. T.
Child.

"Death makes no change in the spirit, morally or
intellectually."—A. R. Wallace.

"No doubt millions of spirits are now pursuing,
practically, earthly careers, drinking and pursuing
evil or sensous courses."—John Wetherby.

"The spirit world is as full of liars as this."—Pom-
eroy's Democrat.

Says Laura Cuppy Smith: "Like attracts like.
When, therefore, a visible scamp with a heart full
of mischief, asks for revelations, he may get them

from the invisible scamp, but their authenticity is deserving of no more credit than the dispatches of some daily papers."

Henry Ward Beecher, in a sermon on the ministry of spirits, vindicating their presence and interest in all our affairs, and invoking the "angels of light," traces the moral effects of a perverted earth-life into the future, and logically and scripturally comes to the conclusion that there are mischievious spirits returning to us:

"Our field of conflict is different from that on which men oppose each other. It comprises the whole unseen realm. All the secret roads, and paths, and avenues, in which spirits dwell, are filled with a great, invisible host. These are our adversaries. And they are all the more dangerous because they are invisible. Subtle are they? We are unconscious of their presence. They come, they go; they assail, they retreat; they plan, they attack, they withdraw; they carry on all the processes by which they mean to suborn or destroy us, without the possibility of our seeing them. When, in physical warfare, the enemy that lies over against us establishes the line of a new redoubt, we can see that; and when a new battery is discovered, a battery may be planted opposite to it; but no engineering can trace these invisible engineers, or their work. And there is· something very august in the thought that the most transcendent powers in the universe, that fill time and space, are removed from the ordinary sight and inspection of men. It is a sublime and awful conception.

It produces some such impression on my mind as is
produced by the idea of haunted houses.

* * * * * *

" There are many who no not believe that this world
is the sphere of evil spirits. They do not believe that
the heaven above is haunted; nor that the world
beneath is haunted; nor that laws, and customs, and
usages, and pleasures, and various pursuits are haunted.
They do not believe in the doctrine of the possession
of spirits. Nevertheless, I confess to you, there is
something in my mind of sublimity in the idea that
the world is full of spirits, good and evil, that are pursuing their various errands, and that the little that we
can see with these bat's eyes of ours, the little that we
can decipher with these imperfect senses, is not the
whole of the reading of those vast pages of that great
volume which God has written. There is in the lore
of God more than our philosophy has ever dreamed of."

Mr. Beecher maintains that spirits are at work on
" the passions, the tastes and sentiments;" that they
have " possession of the great facts, and events, and
constituted agencies of this world "—social, political,
and religious: " No man is a sensible man who says
that the doctrine of evil spirits is a mere superstitious
notion, and treats it as such. It is a reality—an
august reality; and every man who values his soul,
and who has a sense of manhood and immortality,
should take care how he indulges in light, casual, tri-
fling thoughts on this subject, and give heed to such
solemn words as those which were uttered by that hon-

est, truth-speaking man, Paul, when he said, 'We wrestle not against flesh and blood, but against principalities, against powers, against the rulers of the darkness of this world, against spirits of wickedness in heavenly places.'"

MURDEROUS SPIRITS.

The author of the work entitled "The Hereafter," relates the following:

"During the spring of 1871, I received a number of letters from Morgan Reese, Esq., of Higginsville, Illinois, inviting me to come to that place and witness the manifestations in the presence of his daughters. Being compelled to go through Danville, Illinois, twelve miles south of Higginsville, in June of that year, I yielded to his wishes and went to the place. The result of that visit was written up for the *Crucible:*

"The readers of the *Crucible* have already heard somewhat of the astonishing manifestations of this place, but we confess 'the half had not been told.' We went there very doubtful, and told them that we wanted them to do their best, as we wished it for the benefit of the public. The mediums were two daughters of Mr. Morgan Reese, Ardilla and Elizabeth, and William Stump. We had been there but a short time when we heard a voice somewhere—it seemed just beyond, and yet it was near—a voice which sounded somewhat like the voice of a whip-poor-will, which we could understand with great difficulty, and yet it seemed easy for the mediums to understand every word. The voice purported to come from a spirit, and threatened, whether in a joke or not they hardly seemed to understand, to 'draw blood.' This threat had been made so often, and the butcher-knife had been thrown so dangerously near the mediums, that the family, fearing that the spirit may be in earnest about the matter, have locked it up in a drawer, where they seem to think it is beyond his reach. In answer to our inquiries, the spirit said his name was John Richeson; that he murdered his wife over thirty years ago, and hung in Covington, Indiana. He says he is in hell, and we had hard work to convince him that he might progress out of the darkness which then surrounded him.

" We remained there the whole day, and talked with the spirit constantly. One of the mediums played on a jewsharp, when it seemed that a full set were out on the floor dancing, keeping perfect time with the music. All this was in broad daylight, with all the doors open, and the dancing might have been heard several rods from the house.

" While the spirits were talking, objects were constantly flying about the house, kitchen, and even yard— objects of every description, such as the hammer, a saucer, knives, an ear of corn, an iron bar, an ax, and an old chair flying across the yard, and other objects too numerous to mention. At one time, when objects were flying about the house in a most lively manner, a cat, which was about half way across the kitchen, between the room and kitchen doors, was picked up by an unseen hand, and thrown so hard against the open door as to glance off into the yard, about six feet from the kitchen. The cat raised her tail and the hair on her back, and looked back, first on one side, and then on the other, to see who had been facilitating her locomotion, while the spirit and the spectators were all enjoying a hearty laugh over the matter (for the spirit often laughs when he throws objects so near as to frighten persons). Doubtless her feline worship was looking which way to run in order to evade the danger.

" We returned in the evening after the lecture, when the room was made dark, and we never experienced anything so terrific in our life. While the spirit is repeating his threats to 'draw blood,' they are hammering away as if they would batter the house down; objects are thrown all about the house, on the floor, to the great danger of our heads, and the severe detriment of our shins. In the midst of this din and confusion heavy steps are heard, a scuffling ensues, the mediums are calling for lights; but before we can strike our matches they are thrown heavily against the side of the house. This was such a dread reality that it was with difficulty that the mediums could be persuaded to allow the light extinguished again."

NEW ZEALAND MAORIS.

During our recent travels and labors in New Zealand we had frequent opportunities of learning about the religious views of the semi-civilized Maoris, the original Polygamous inhabitants of this island—a people who have rapidly degenerated since the advent there of Christian missionaries. And here, as in all lands of our travels, were we reminded of the spiritual degrees of humanity, each having its abuses of gifts involving the obsessional influences common to all ages.

These New Zealand Maoris believed in a plurality of invisible gods, and a future existence, although the *tapu* took the place of religious observances. They had priests and " sorcerers," and held intercourse with their " ancestral dead." They were troubled with demons. The heads of the chiefs were tabooed (*tapu*), no one being allowed to touch them, or hardly allude to them, under fearful penalties. They believed in charms, and wore them. Death, to them, was the passage to the *Reinga*, the unseen world, or place of departed spirits. They did not fear to die, yet preferred living in their mortal bodies. They believed that individuals occupied different apartments in *Reinga*, according as their earthly lives had been good or ill. Messages were frequently given to dying persons to take to deceased relatives in this shadow-land of souls. All of their funeral wails over their recent dead ended with, "Go! go, dear one, away to thy people!" It is a singular coincidence that the Fijians, Tahitians, Tongans, and Samoans, as well as the New Zealanders, considered the place of departure of the spirits, on their way to the unseen world, as the western extremities of their islands.

Relation to, and communion with, a world of spirits are beliefs almost if not completely universal. The native tribes and clans of these islands are not only aware of holding intercourse with the so-called dead, but they understand the abuse, often using their mediumistic privileges for selfish ends. During their wars with the English, they were uniformly made acquainted by vision, clairvoyance, or clairaudience, with the movements of the British troops before action in battle. Not a plan of Her Majesty's officers could be kept from them. The leading chief of the *Han Hans* was a noted medium and medicine-man. He distinctly said that the " spirits of the dead " guided him to his victories. The Maoris in the north island still own much territory, have their king, and hold but little intercourse with *pakeha*, the white man.

The medium-priest in a tribe is called *Tohunga*. They meet in close apartments, and chant their songs till the flickering fire fades away, when the *Tohunga* goes into his ecstatic state, and the spirit controlling tenders council, describes his new habitation in spirit-life, gives the names of those whom he has met, and bears messages in return to kindred in the higher life.

A REMARKABLE CASE.

Mr. W. B——, residing in San Francisco, is a gentleman of thought and intelligence. He was our chief engineer on board the steamer Nevada, from the Sandwich Islands to New Zealand. Learning of our being a Spiritualist, he fully unbosomed himself, giving the following cases of obsession in his family. This is the substance of his statement:

Himself, wife and family had often heard of Spiritualism; but had never attended a lecture, a circle, or read a book upon the subject. Like others, they supposed it a delusion, and beneath their notice. A few years since, when property was rising, Mr. B—— bought a house on Green street, and moved into it. He had no knowledge of the family of whom he had purchased, or of the previous one that had there resided. He had been in the house hardly four weeks when his daughter, a girl of thirteen years of age, while playing on the piano one evening, hesitated, became a little spasmodic, and partly leaned over upon the piano. Mr. B—— spoke to her. No reply. He spoke again; "Carrie! *Carrie!*" No answer. A little alarmed, he went to her, and could hardly lift her hands from the piano. They seemed cold, clammy, and adhered to the instrument. He took her in his arms and laid her upon the sofa, when she began to make the deaf and dumb alphabet. It surprised the parents; for, though they knew something of the deaf and dumb alphabet by seeing it talked, they could not understand what was said by the intelligence. Puzzled—resolved to keep the family secret—Mr. B—— procured a deaf and dumb alphabet, with explanations, and by the aid of the spirit he soon learned to talk with the controlling intelligence. The daughter was totally unconscious. She always thought, when coming out of the trance, that she had fallen asleep. The parents were careful not to mention spirits or Spiritualism to her, though they were becoming deeply interested in a subject which they had considered trickery and chicanery. Carrie continued in school, yet fell into this trance every evening, talking through the deaf and dumb alphabetic motions. Mr. B—— became quite an expert in this language, and was attached to the deaf and dumb spirit.

Five weeks had now elapsed, when one evening about the usual time of the entrancement, she seemed going into the condition; but the manner, the motions, the appearance, were all different. At length she began to talk—fluently, but incoherently. It was evidently a different spirit. Night after night the new intelligence came, controlling the daughter. She would walk her about the room very familiarly, but positively refused to give her name. The family became quite spiritualistic—in private. The spirit seemed talkative and rather pleasant, unless crossed, when she would rage most fearfully. Mrs. B—— would reprove her, which only intensified her anger, and made her take a dislike to her.

A few of the neighbors coming in, said, "Why, Carrie (the daughter) walks, talks, and acts precisely like Miss ——, who died in this house, and was such a bad character! She died about two years ago; was eighteen years old, was very rough, had an illegitimate child, and when angry, would rave and curse."

Hearing of the case, the Catholics in an adjoining street, said "it is the devil;" and one evening brought

in some flasks containing holy water wherewith to
"lay the devil." The spirit said, "Come to cast out a
demon, have you, with holy water? I'll show you!"
And seizing the bottle of the water smashed it into a
thousand pieces. Mrs. B—— reproved her—slapped
her hands. The spirit, sneeringly grinning, said, "slap
away, you don't hurt me any; you only hurt *your
child*."

Mrs. Birdsall disliked the controlling spirit, and
began, because of this influence, to take a dislike to
Spiritualism, although she was becoming something
of a medium herself.

Ere long the Rev. Dr. Elliot heard of the strange
manifestations, or demoniac control, and begged of
Mr. B——, the father, to let him come in sometime.
Mr. B—— asked the spirit, who said, "What has he
got to do with me? No, I don't want to see him."

But the reverend gentleman was anxious to see this
strange trance medium—a mere child.

Finally Mr. B—— invited the clergyman in.
The spirit was controlling the medium. The doctor
said, "Carrie, do you say your prayers?"

The intelligence said, "Speak to me; Carrie is
unconscious."

"Well," said the minister, "do *you* say your
prayers?"

"None of your business, sir. What do you want
of *me* anyway?"

The clergyman took down the Bible and began to
read the Scriptures, when she burst out in a rage, say-

ing, "By what authority do you come here to read the
Bible to me? Leave the house!"

Mr. Elliot kept on reading, when she seized a chair
and rushed for him; and as he hurried down stairs she
struck him quite severely in the back, and then started
for the lamp, evidently designing to dash it upon his
head, when he rushed out of doors and left.

Mr. B——, meeting the clergyman a few days after,
asked him if he wished to see the manifestations again.
"No, *no*," said he; "I believe that spirit would knife
me were I to go there again."

A skeptic suggested that the daughter might be
deceiving her parents. The spirit exclaimed, "You
are a fool! You, Mr. William L. —— (giving the
full name), are a bad man;" and then revealed his
life, shaking her finger, saying, "I know more; I
know all about you." The man was glad to get away.
She would also expose others' secrets when reproved.
To a woman she said, "Madam, I know you. You
better not have that soldier come to your house so
much when your husband is away. I know your whole
history, I do."

Mrs. B——, believing Spiritualism is all diabolical,
tried to drive that spirit away, then would coax and
plead, but all to no purpose. Only abuse would follow the attempt—so extreme they did not dare to have
any of the neighbors come in.

At times the spirit controlling would cause Carrie to
sit as in a sullen meditation, moaning in most pitiful
tones, saying, "My child, oh my child! can't you bring

me my child?" Sometimes Carrie would be under this control all day; and toward evening the intelligence would take this child medium up in her best room, putting on all the jewelry she could find, and insist upon going to the theater. Mr. B —— would go with her, converse with her between the acts, etc. In the morning Carrie would know nothing of it.

Mr. Jackson, a clairvoyant now in San Francisco, whom we met several times, called to see this obsessed girl. The spirit told him of a transaction that occurred about the time of his landing in the city. He never called again. Whenever she came out of this trance state, she (the girl) was hungry, and must always have something to eat.

Mrs. B——, while shopping one day, lost the diamond from her ring. It was very valuable, and she was feeling sad, when this spirit entranced Carrie and said, "*I can find your ring!*" and beckoned her to follow her and the medium. Mrs. B—— did so, and was directed straight to the diamond, and found it where she had taken off her glove.

When this spirit dressed this girl up to go out, she would put all the jewelry on that she could find, and if she could not get enough she would steal it. The spirit was very fond of the opera, the theater, of jewelry, and gadding in the streets. The neighbors all said that jewelry, and theaters, and dance-houses were among the chief attractions of the unfortunate woman that lived and died there a year or two ago.

Mr. B—— would sometimes start with his daugh-

8

ter for the theater, and on the way this spirit would take control, and Mr. B——— could not drive nor coax her to leave. If he strenuously reproved or threatened this spirit, she would curse and swear, and throw her down into the streets. Several times the spirit threw her down into the streets, and Mr. B——— has had to take her up in his arms and carry her to an office, or to her home.

The spirit always said she did not want to *hurt* the girl, but did want to torment the *child's mother*. There were spirits, she said, who owed her a grudge, and they said, " We can only get at *her* through the child! "

This spirit would sometimes quite despair, saying, " I'm miserable here in this dark sphere, and can't get out of it. I feel better when I get hold of the medium. I was a hard case on earth, and now I mean to get my revenge." * * *

Mr. B——— was of the opinion, as the control became more easy by oft repeating, that the spirit made some progress. Selling out and leaving that house, the obsession was nearly broken up by his putting his daughter under the supervision of a family of mediumistic and positive Spiritualists of orderly spheres.

CASE OF A UNIVERSALIST MINISTER.

Rev. B. S. Hobbs, of New York State, well known there for his mediumistic experiences while a Universalist clergyman, communicated a letter to the *Ban-*

ner of Light a few years before his departure for the spirit life, in which he said:

"More than once has my speech been controlled in the presence of my audience, while engaged in the sacred service of public prayer; and by the strangest demonstration, I have been prevented from repeating the service, until at last I was compelled to use the Liturgy; much painful, *tried* experience, rendering extempore prayer literally impossible. More than once, also, have I been driven from the workshop, after being forced, for a time, by positive control, to leave the pulpit. This to me is not easy of solution. It seems like violence which no spirit is justified in inflicting on a mortal. And were it not for my own personal *tried* experience, I should not believe it even possible.

"On three Sabbaths, two of them in succession, I have, although in a usual state of health, been prevented by that kind of control which some, termed 'mediums,' if not others, will understand. I have been prevented from speaking a word for hours, and been otherwise thus influenced as to make the usual performance of my Sabbath duties literally and to me, after much effort and trial, clearly impossible.

"Again, then, I am in fact, literally driven from the pulpit, though happily saved from a public exhibition before my audience, few of whom, if indeed any, are conversant with the manifestations termed spirit influence on the human system."

Mr. Hobbs used to come to our house (Junior Editor's), in Oswego, immediately after being released from the Lunatic Asylum. He said he was no more insane when thus in Utica, than when in our room; but only under the control of different orders of spirits. The lower order, when obsessing him, would throw his awls out of his hands in his shoemaker's shop, throw the hammer from his hand, throw the Bible off from the pulpit when he was preaching, make him froth at the mouth, swear like a "piper," and then compose psalms. He would actually improvise psalms in the style of David's, that no one could tell from David's, so far as *style* and *diction* were concerned. Poor man! He was open to *all* kinds of control. Some were good, and then he was beautiful; but they tore his nervous system all to tatters. He, of course, was unwise, but did the best he knew.

This is not an isolated case. There are wrecks, shattered wrecks of sensitives known as mediums, all through the land. Some of these constitutionally unfitted for the reception of the magnetic stimulus, have persistently given themselves up to a sort of medium-mania till their nervous systems are only comparable to "reeds shaken with the wind."

DIVINATION.

This art of discovering things secret or future by certain signs, reviving these days in more general use, was anciently practiced as a science in different systems or methods; as, for instance, *Aeromancy*, divining by the air; *Arithmancy*, by means of numbers; *Capnomancy*, by the smoke of sacrifices; *Chiromancy*, by lines on the palms of the hands; *Hydromancy*, by water; *Pyromancy*, by fire; *Ophiomancy*, by serpents; *Necromancy*, by visiting tombs; *Belomancy*, by arrows, etc. The so-called *wizards* and *witches* divined also by the flights of birds, by clouds, eclipses, transits of stars, rods, lots, images, cups, etc. These arts were common with the ancient inhabitants of Palestine, Egypt, Caldea, Arabia, and other Oriental countries. The professors of augurs and soothsayings were consulted in the most ordinary as well as the most important occurrences of life. Regarded with a feeling of awe by the superstitious masses, these media at length instituted a religion of their own, with pompous and imposing ceremonies. Voudouism, as practiced by African tribes, and in our Southern country, is but a form of divination. Their fetish images placed at the door of those they would injure or obsess, working to a charm on superstitious and negative people, are but the agencies of magnetizing. A will-force exerted upon the distant parties in direct concentration would be more effectual.

Dr. P. B. Randolph, who has made himself " master of secret arts," and whose observations and experiences with the Voudous of New Orleans, Long Island, and of foreign countries, are extensive, speaks of the magic power of twin rings and amulets, and avers "it is possible to prepare and charge certain materials so that they will retain the *nerváura* of one person and impart it to another, kindling up magnetic love between them,

just as a little yeast will leaven a whole barrel of flour."
He also says " he has known these arts to be practiced
for purposes of lust, passion, revenge, love, and pecu-
niary speculation, with a strange and horrible success.
* * * But such obfuscation can easily be overcome
by a timely resort to magnetic magic of a higher
grade."

Moral character having nothing to do with this
divining system of mediumship, we could expect nothing from it but a jumble of signs and conclusions, with
orgies and sensualities most polluting. Only the light
of science can cull out whatever fact is here embodied.
Only the culture of moral responsibilities in spiritual
revealments — thus inviting the guardianship and
inspiration of wise spirits — can render divination
reliable and worthy of private or public trust.

DEVELOPMENT AND DEGENERATION.

In connection with Mr. Darwin's theory of "Development," Dr. Laycock's theory of "Degeneration"
seems to be deserving of attention and candid examination. In a sense the two theories may be regarded
as complimentary to each other, the same subject being
contemplated, as it were, by the one from a synthetical
and by the other from an analytical point of view. As
professor of the practice of medicine and clinical medicine, and lecturer on medical psychology and mental
disease, in the University of Edinburgh, Dr. Laycock
speaks with some authority. Mr. Darwin has attempted
to trace the general ascent of man through various

stages of the animated series. Dr. Laycock seeks to establish the partial descent of man once again to certain of these stages. According to him the principle by which diseases, both bodily and mental, are to be explained and classified, is that they are the results of processes by which function, structure, and organ change in an order the reverse of evolution. Hence it follows that phenomena indicative of abnormal conditions in human beings, are phenomena indicative of normal conditions in inferior organizations. "Thus," says Dr. Laycock, "in the degenerations of the blood of man the normal types of the blood-corpuscle of the lower vertebrates appear as the degenerate white corpuscles of *leukamia*, and the abnormal production of uric acid as urates in certain diseases has its counterpart in the normal production in birds and reptiles. So also with other morbid products, as sugar, glucose, starch, fats, oxalic acid, and the like, that which is morbid in man is normal lower down in the scale. Not otherwise is the law of cerebral functional activity and mental qualities."

According to this the blood, by certain habits, is degenerated and animalized. As the body, with all its organs, is the evolution of the blood, its magnetic sphere will be correspondingly debased and gross. As the physical body is correlated with the spiritual, it (the spiritual) will thus be tainted, or more or less darkened and deflected to the earthly and sensual, making thus a complete habitual self-pollution in every part. It is said that soldiers starving to death, lose their rationality at a certain stage, and owing to the condition of their blood, become ferocious as wild beasts. In such instances, doubtless, the spirit, famishing, withdraws to save a greater wreck, leaving the earthly man but a mere irrational animal. So if the spirit be starved by vicious habits, a similar result must follow.

Syphilis, and other diseases, are communicated by sexual and other methods of contact. The sexual, being the life-batteries, the very fountain of physical and mental supply, must, of course, when tainted or poisoned by what cannot be appropriated, or by what is magnetically repellant, or any way diseased, be polluted thereby in blood, and thence in the whole sphere, thus allying that person with sensual association as by force till made a wreck of health or hope. Spirits of like demands are in this ring, procuring their gratification by magnetic imbibation! How do we affect spirits then? How do they affect us? As this world is fundamental physically, as the base of support to the next, the redemption of unfortunate spirits living in our magnetic atmosphere depends much upon our habits of life.

HELLISH ORGIES.

One of the greatest possible evidences of magnetic pollution and phantasy, is a self-praise of purity and a claim of being honored with lofty spirits. When persons are so sure that no spirits inspire them but the good and great—such as Jesus, Plato, Washington, and the like—it is certain a deception lurks somewhere in their affections. If a *child* spirit is our guardian angel, we can thus learn wisdom, for "of such is the kingdom of heaven."

There are other phases of obsession equally demoralizing. Spiritualism has had its *seances* ranging no higher than mundane psychology; pretentious entrancements to tickle the fancy of the curious crowd; tricksters by the wholesale; the psychic nausea of sensational banquets; a spiritual auction for legerdemain; a sentimental empiricism, and as frequently a leadership making "merchandise of the kingdom of heaven." Nor is this the all of a wide-spread obsession. There is a vice that fruits legitimately from this indiscriminate invite to all sorts of psychological influences from "the good, bad and indifferent,"—that *incidental* vice, that open gateway to the hells!

And yet there are blinded souls who, shrinking from physical promiscuity, seek to satiate the morbid desires of their inverted mental states by magnetic promiscuity, ever hankering for "pawing" mediums, and even non-mediums must magnetize them. This intermixing of discordant magnetic influences invites disorderly-inclined spirits. The results are deplorable.

If physical promiscuity destroys the body, magnetic promiscuity destroys the healthy activities of the soul. Thus are both soul and body "cast into hell"—that hell of inharmony where the "worm" of remembrance dieth not, and the "fire" of remorse is not quenched.

There are cases parallel in modern times with what

9

the Bible speaks of—a carnal intercourse with infesting spirits. Israel was warned lest their sons and daughters might "go whoring after the gods" of the Canaanites—a habit they actually practiced, according to the record (Judges ii: 17). The holy angels are careful what spheres they touch. There is such a thing as spiritual adultery. Said the Nazarene: "Whosoever looketh on a woman to lust after her hath committed adultery already with her in his heart."

We have heard of instances where the parties concerned, under the plea to "facilitate the magnetic process," sat at periodic times in a dark circle—men and women perfectly nude! The "manifestations" were, of course, of a grade exactly corresponding with the purpose and associations, being lewd and infestiously beastial.

The beautiful art of healing by the laying-on of hands has also been perverted to the same business, and in a more horrible manner. The statements have come to us by parties conversant with the facts, that certain so-called magnetic healers have decoyed married and unmarried women who applied to them for this curative agency, and made practical their "philosophy of life," as they called it, healing and "developing mediumship" by promiscuous sexual acts! Institutions of this kind have actually been established in some cities of America, and operated for a season, and even advertised awhile in some of the newspapers. Were we not acquainted with persons who have been inmates of such institutions, serving them in the capacity of healers, also testified to by those who visited them, being induced by recommendations of advertised cures, and who revolted at the scenes there enacted, we should doubt the reports of their doings, scarcely believing that human nature could be capable of sinking to so immoral debasement.

It is the opinion of those who have seen for themselves, that the operators of such institutions are *insanely* obsessed on the animal plane, and of course are breaking down physically as well as morally. It may be possible, under the blinding influences of passional magnetisms, that such persons may work their imaginations into a condition of sincerity, and even argue the legitimacy of such conduct. But let the sickly and putrid look of their faces settle this matter; let the miasmatic air that fills such abodes warn the unwary that such is the GATE OF HELL; let the soul's sorrow and shame of those who in their better moments reflect upon life's solemn responsibilities both in habit and example, be as a burning fire in such *Gehennas* of sensuality and dark obsessions.

It requires but little charity to consider the statement of the *Independent* as true, when we reflect that the theology on which it bases its religion is partly the " Patriarchical institution " which it so righteously condemns when patronized to-day. But let the church be credited if it can surpass its theology. At any rate, we endorse what it says respecting the infestations of lustful alliances, and can only hope that the same healthful rebuke my be applied just as vigorously in the sanctuary where the Levites " pervert the ways of the Lord " in secret adulteries:

" It is against the creatures who clothe an abandoned manhood in beastly sweetness of tender demeanor, and make a moral apostleship out of clever luring of female imaginations into dens of desire, which they misname tabernacles of divine love, that good men should invoke all detestation and scorn. Virile qualities were never more degraded than in the masterful licentates who mistake a slop of animal sentiment for a well of water springing up unto everlasting life, and sink in the bottomless bog of demoralized passion with cries of glory unto the rock on which their feet are planted."

Nor is it any apology for any of us in this age of enlightenment to practice deception or adultery in or out of the church because the Hebrew Lord encouraged a lying spirit:

" And he said, Hear thou therefore the word of the Lord: I saw the Lord sitting on his throne, and all the host of heaven standing by him on his right hand and on his left. And the Lord said, Who shall persuade Ahab, that he may go up and fall at Ramoth-gilead? And one said on this manner, and another said on that manner. And there came forth a spirit, and stood before the Lord, and said, I will persuade him. And the Lord said unto him, Wherewith? And he said, I will go forth, and I will be a lying spirit in the mouth of all his prophets. And he said, Thou shalt persuade him, and prevail also: go forth and do so. Now therefore, behold, the Lord hath put a lying spirit in the mouth of all these thy prophets, and the Lord hath spoken evil concerning thee."—1 Kings xxii.

Nay, our moral obligations are more than Hebraic; more than Christian, which rejoiced where sin abounded that grace might much more abound! Zoroaster, in the Zend Avesta, taught what we all endorse, that self-abnegation is the path to paradise: "Avoid licentiousness, because it is one of the readiest means to give evil spirits power over body and soul. Strive, therefore, to keep pure in body and mind, and thus prevent the entrance of evil spirits, who are always trying to gain possession of man. To think evil is a sin."

CHAPTER V.

A WITCH was an ignorant instrument in the hands of the demons, while a magician was their master by means of a science known only to the few. In the earlier ages of Christianity this mysterious science (now entitled Spiritism) flourished widely; there were noted schools of magic in different parts of Europe. The witch always remained the same poor and despised outcast from among her fellow-creatures; whilst the magician, using the same laws with better understanding, was a man of power, having wonderful control over the superstitious masses. This masculine prerogative was owing to man's accredited superiority of rights—rights of brute force!

The intoxication of this mental hydrophobia called witchcraft, was often induced by artificial stimulants. The Thracians used to intoxicate themselves by casting the seeds of certain poisonous plants into a fire made for the purpose, around which they sat and inspired the narcotic fumes. Moore says that there can be no doubt that the incantations of witchcraft and magic were generally attended with the practice of burning herbs of a similar kind. The ancients deemed certain temperaments essential to the reception of the divine

(102)

afflatus, and the melancholic were considered the most suitable, especially when aggravated by rigid abstinence and the use of narcotics (this exactly suits Swedenborg, etc.). Pliny informs us that the soothsayers were accustomed to chew roots supposed to be of a certain species of henbane. The Hindoos employ the Indian hemp for the same purpose; in St. Domingo the supposed prophets chew a plant called cohaba; and the Fetish tribes of Africa drink their poisonous libations to spirits. In our own day we have known of cases where some of our would-be Spiritual speakers have entranced themselves by harshish and ether in order to be abnormal before an eager crowd of sensationalists in quest of a sign of spirit control!

THE AFRICAN CAMMA.

Superstitious people are negatives; their simple faith cultivates mediumship. Hence, the ruder, ignorant tribes are spiritually minded, in their way, having close intercourse with spirits of a like grade, who naturally linger near the earth with their old associations, every day and night seen and heard by their prophets. The Camma and other African tribes aver they " hear ghosts speaking "—their own departed relatives—who say they " are tired of living in the bush " (burying grounds) " and want their friends to build them a little house by the town." This done, the spirits enter there and manifest themselves in strange, yet recognizable ways.

BIBLICAL WITCHCRAFT.

Witchcraft, being a disorderly mediumship, has been

considered by all superstitious people the work of an evil genius; by many Christians, attributed to the devil. Hence laws and terrible penalties, and sacrificial deaths to exterminate the witches. Here is exhibited the Hebrew code so malignant. It seems the ancient Canaanites practiced witchcraft, and it continued with the Israelites through all their journeyings, of which the honest "woman of Endor" is an example:

" When thou art come into the land which the Lord thy God giveth thee, thou shalt not learn to do after the abominations of those nations. There shall not be found among you any one that maketh his son or his daughter to pass through the fire, or that useth divination, or an observer of the times, or an enchanter, or a witch, or a charmer, or a consulter with *familiar spirits*, or a wizzard, or a *necromancer*. For all that do these things are an abomination unto the Lord."— Deuteronomy xviii: 9–12.

" Regard not them that have familiar spirits, neither seek after wizzards, to be defiled by them: I am the Lord your God."—Leviticus xix: 31.

ECCLESIASTIC PERSECUTION.

How black is Ecclesiastic history dating from this Biblical law! No sooner had King James ascended the throne than there was issued a formal declaration against religious toleration. Not content with this, he put forth laws decidedly unjust against witchcraft and witches; and Parliament was so shamefully subservient to this monarch, that from his coming into power to the latter portion of the 17th century, the enormous number of three thousand one hundred and ninety-two individuals were condemned and executed in Great Britain alone, under the accusation of witchcraft, sorcery, and conjuration.

Had the people of this time understood mental science, mesmerism, biology, psychological impression, and the laws of mediumship, those wholesale murders, under cover of Christianity, would never have stained the pages of English history. And if in our times these laws are not better understood, who shall guarantee us exemption from a similar martyrdom? The times portend such a repetition of history!

In an interesting chapter on sorcery and witchcraft, Lecky says: "Tens of thousands of victims perished by the most agonizing and protracted torments. * * * In almost every province of Germany, but especially where Ecclesiastic influence predominated, the persecution raged with fearful intensity. Seven thousand victims are said to have been burned at Trèves. In France decrees were passed on the subject by the Parliaments of Paris, Toulouse, Bordeaux, Rheims, Rowen, Dijon, and Rennes, and they were all followed by a harvest of blood. The executions which took place in Paris were, in the emphatic words of an old writer, 'almost infinite.' * * * In Italy, a thousand persons were executed in a single year in the province of Como; and in other parts of the country the severity of the Inquisitions at last created an absolute rebellion." — *Rationalism in Europe*, *Vol.* 1, *pp.* 28–31.

Nor was the persecution exclusively Catholic. In Luther's "Table Talk," (1538) we find this: "The talk falling on witches who spoil eggs, etc., Luther said, 'I should have no compassion on these witches; I would burn them.'"—p. 251. Calvin illustrated the same law and spirit in the burning of Servetus at the stake. In Protestant England and Scotland, more especially during the Seventeenth century, witches were pursued at times with an implacable fury. There are instances of witch-burning less than a hundred years ago, in Spain. "In 1773, the Divines of the Associated Presbytery (Scotland) passed a resolution declaring their faith in witchcraft, and deploring the growing skepticism on the subject." — *Macaulay's History of England*, *Vol.* 3, *p.* 706.

The New England witchcraft, that casts to this day a horrid light over Puritanical history, is another phase of Spiritualism, mostly on the obsessional plane, and so diabolically managed by the church as to "confound saints and sinners." As we look back upon the visitation of the spirits to the colonies, and note the most horrible abuse of their influences, by the clergy principally, we cannot help feeling, if there be any "devils," they have a long account to settle with the witch murderers of New England.

MAYLAY WITCHES.

During our travels among the Maylay tribes, we had frequent occasion to observe the effects of superstitious ideas upon the ignorant masses, producing a species of witchcraft.

In the Thirteenth century Mohammedan missionaries converted the Malays in the Straits of Malacca to Islamism, using persuasion instead of the sword. Their original religion, however, was entirely different. John Cameron, F. R. G. S., assures us that "such Malays as have embraced none of the more modern religions believe in some Divine Personality, corresponding to God, and a future life, where good men enjoy ecstatic bliss, and the wicked suffer purgatorial punishments." But "their religion," he adds, "is strangely mixed up with *demonology*. They believe that every person is attended by a good and bad angel; the latter leading to sickness, danger, and sin, while the good angel seeks the individual's health and happiness." In their "lives, they are influenced more by fear than hope." They propitiate the wicked angel and the evil spirits. It is only at death that they ask the especial care of their good angel. They stand in no fear of the transition. Some of their ruins indicate a relationship theologically to the sun and "serpent worshipers."

All that witchcraft amounts to is simply a mixed control, arising generally, first, from perverted conditions of body; and second, from the pyschic influence of superstitious minds, both in and out of the body. It frequently occurs these days. All that is wanted is a little light on the subject.

HALLUCINATIONS.

As yet we know but little of the process of electro-photographing upon the brain. Thus far it is ascertained, however, that the images of things and thoughts are there retained, even when, for the time being, the same may be forgotten, but afterwards, with years intervening, they are called up in all their original freshness as if real. The brain is a living canvas on which is limned all we have seen, heard, felt, thought of. "It possesses the latent power of adjusting in consecutive order, by the co-action of its organs, whatever imaging of idea is impressed upon it. A single sensation or emotion may give rise to wonderful picturings of fancy. Dreams, for instance, may originate in some outward physical condition. A person sleeping in the cold may as likely as not dream of freezing in a snowdrift; and if ignorant, may perhaps on the morrow believe that he is fated to die so the very next winter."

In their simple-mindedness many have accepted all unseen influences and their phenomena as angel ministries, and followed such promptings into the most idle vagaries—all in the name of Spiritualism. Fancies of thought, dreams, day reveries, mental abstractedness, and other involuntary flashes of brain, produced as likely as not by certain habits of body, diseases, or spheral reflections from associations, have all been reckoned by credulous Spiritualists as voices from the spirits! With no appeal to reason or common sense philosophy of mind, they of course get bewildered.

In certain states of the atmosphere, by the laws of refraction, the images of objects will rise up and appear to be real. Travelers are often deceived thereby. We mirror our own inner condition. Beware how we follow this mirage of mental inversion.

> "Oh, fly the glimmer of those haunted plains,
> Whereon the demon of delusion reigns."

Beware of a self-deception! The condition of the soul is most lamentable when, from the specious logic, breeding a corresponding habit, it deludes itself with the obsessional idea that all human impulses are orderly and should be obeyed as legitimate. There can be no lower hell to the soul than when it embosoms in its trust all that comes to it. Is every whim of a child to be indulged? Is every feeling a practical utility? There are high courts within us where all emotions, voices, desires, prayers, hopes, aspirations, are to be weighed and balanced. It is madness to be deadened to our relations in life under pretense of an absorbed spirituality and superior attainment. There can be no worse impoverishment. To be spiritual is to be rational, reasonable, practical. Every sense must have a life intensity; every intellectual and moral force awakened up to the sharpest criticism to prove all things.

CHAPTER VI.

EFFECTS OF ASSOCIATIONS.

THE human mind, more readily the mediumistic, transfers its states to the objects it inspects, and these states may be induced at first by association.

Speaking of Luther, the *Christian Union* says: "His early life among the wild mountains and in the mines had imbued his mind with superstitious fears of unseen powers; and there was little in the religious life of the age to counterbalance such conceptions. His logic never became thorough master of his imagination; and in this light we must always estimate Luther. Devils, to him, were as real as human beings; and his conflicts with them were genuine."

A Greek gentleman residing on the spot once so venerated as the seat of divine inspiration, where the Pythia proved her power of foretelling events, furnishes some interesting descriptions of the place, together with notices of the wild region which was the scene of the Cumæan Sibyl's vaticinations. This writer says:

"The Lake of Avernus was once the extinct crater of a mighty volcano, and the whole region, though now fertilized by its waters, bears the marks of being fire-scarred, and presents a most gloomy and repulsive

appearance. The clefts in the savage rocks abound
with caverns exhaling mephitic vapors and bitumin-
ous odors. It was in one of the wildest, grandest, yet
most awe-inspiring gorges of these mountains that
the cavern existed which tradition affirms to have been
the dwelling of the Cumæan Sibyl. The scattered
inhabitants of the surrounding district believed that
this gloomy grotto was the entrance to the nether
world; that the hammers of the Titans, working in the
mighty laboratories of the Plutonic realms, might be
heard, ever and anon, reverberating through the thick
and sullen air. The dark waters of the gloomy lake
were supposed to communicate directly with the silent
flow of the river of death, the Lethean stream, made
dreadful by the apparitions of unblest spirits who
floated from the Avernian shores to the realms of
eternal night and torture. Here dwelt the famous
Cumæan Sibyl, and from the exhalations of those poisonous regions, fatal to the birds that attempted to
wing their way through its burdened airs, or the living
creatures that strayed amidst its savage wilds, this
weird woman derived that fierce ecstasy in which she
wrote and raved of the destiny of nations, the fate of
armies, the downfall of kingdoms, and the decay of
dynasties."

There can be no doubt but that the awe of such sol-
itudes was one of the causes of the Pythia's gloomy
descriptions of the spiritual scenery printed psychologically upon her brain, and that such descriptions,
accepted as valid by the Grecian devotees without ques-

tioning analysis, gave to the civilizations of those times their wierd and mysterious characteristics, so forbidding to us tamer philosophers of the Nineteenth century.

How important it is that our media should be enlightened in mental science, and be protectingly guarded against positive magnetic depredations, and surrounded by the most favorable associations and influences, in order to obtain the most natural and happy impressions of spirit entities. The truest and most reliable communications come through well-balanced minds, toned by pure habits to close reasoning, but disciplined also to receptive or negative polarity. Such attract corresponding grades of mind in both worlds, till what we receive so is burnished up with high thought. As in olden times there were "Schools of the Prophets," so should we have departments in our new systems of education for the development and spiritual keeping of mediumship; for the best methods of communication, that they may be fortified against all encroachment upon their rights or consecration to their work.

A LICENTIOUS MEDIUM.

Epes Sargent, in his admirable work entitled "Peculiar," relates an incident of mediumistic life, perfectly illustrative of this law, wherein is portrayed the facility with which a negative mind is swayed by its surroundings. Peek, in quest of his stolen wife (during the last days of slavery in the late Rebellion) applies to J. Bender, consulting medium. Bender is a young man, dirty, shabby, intemperate, licentious.

"How is business, Mr. Bender?" asked Peek.

"Very slim just now," said Bender. "This war fills people's minds. Can I do anything for you to-day?"

"Yes. You remember the young woman at the house I took you to the other day—the one whose name you said was Clara?"

"I remember. She paid me handsomely. Much obliged to you for taking me. Will you have a sip of Bourbon?"

"No, thank you; I don't believe in anything stronger than water. I want to know if you can tell me where in the city that young lady is."

Bender put down his cigar, clasped his hands, laid them on the table, and closed his eyes. In a minute his whole face seemed transfigured. A certain sensual expression it had worn was displaced by one of rapt and tender interest. The lids of his eyes hung loosely over the uprolled balls. He looked five years younger. He sighed several times heavily, moved his lips and throat as if laboring to speak, and then seemed absorbed as if witnessing unspeakable things. He remained thus four or five minutes, and then put out his hands and placed them on one of Peek's.

"Ah! this is a good hand," said the young seer; "I like the feel of it. I wish his would speak as well of him."

"Of whom do you mean?"

10

"Of this one whose hands are on yours. Ah! he is weak, and you are strong. He knows the right, but he will not do the right. He knows there is a heaven, and yet he walks hellward."

"Can we not save him?" asked Peek.

"No. His own bitter experience must be his tutor."

"Why will he try to deceive?" asked Peek; "to deceive sometimes, even in these manifestations of his wonderful gift?"

"You see it is the very condition of that gift that he should be impressible to influences, whether good or bad. He takes his color from the society which encamps around him. Sometimes, as now, the good ones come, and then so bitterly he bewails his faults. Sometimes the bad get full possession of him, and he is what they will—a drunkard, a liar, a thief, a scoffer. Yes, I have known him to scoff at those great facts which make spirit existence to him a certainty."

"Can I help him in any way? Will money aid him to throw off the bad influences?"

"No. Poor as he is, he has too much money. He does not know the true uses of it. He must learn them through suffering. Leave him to the discipline of the earth-life. You know what that is. How much you must have passed through. How sad, and yet how brave and cheerful you have been! It all comes to me as I press the palm of your hand. Ah! you have sought her so long and earnestly! and you cannot find her! and you think she is faithful to you still!"

" Yes, and neither mortal nor spirit can make me think otherwise. But tell me where I shall look for her."

The young man lifted the black hand to his white forehead and pressed the palm there for a moment, and then, with a sigh, laid it gently on the table and said: " It is of no use. I get confused impressions—nothing clear or forcible. Why have you not consulted me before about your wife?"

" Because, first, I wished to leave it to you to find out what I wanted; and this you have done at last. Secondly, I did not think I could trust you, or rather the intelligence that might speak through you. But you have been more candid than I expected. You have not pretended, as you often do, to more knowledge than you really possess."

" The reason is that I am now admitted into a state where I can look down on myself as from a higher plane; so that I feel like a different being from myself, and must distinguish between *me* as I now *am*, and *him* as he usually *is*." [What a solemn truth is here! what a contemplation for a spirit to see itself mirrored in a medium—darkly when that medium is surrounded by evil influences—light and beautiful when surrounded by the good!]

" Do you know what is truly the hell of evil doers? *It is to see themselves* as they are, *and God as he is.* These tame preachers rave about hell-fire and lakes of sulphur. What poor, feeble, halting imaginations they have! Better beds of brimstone than a couch of

down on which one lies seeing what one might have
been, but is not—than seeing what he *is*."

[The medium then gave Peek a slight clue to his
wife, which, when followed out, in due time led to her
discovery. The spirit requested him to pay Bender
two dollars only, " not a cent more."]

The clairvoyant sighed heavily, and leaning his
elbows on the table, covered his face with his hands.
He remained in this posture for nearly a minute.
Suddenly he dropped his hands, shook himself, and
started up. His eyes were open. He stared wildly
about, then seemed to slip back into his old self. The
former unctious, villainous expression returned to his
face. He looked around for his half-smoked cigar,
which he took up and re-lighted. Peek drew two
dollars from a purse, and offered them to him.

" I reckon you can afford more than that," said Mr.
Bender.

" That is your regular fee," replied Peek; " I haven't
been here half an hour."

" Oh, well, we won't dispute about it," said the
medium, thrusting the rags into a pocket of his vest.

THE GAMBLER'S DEN.

The following incident of actual occurrence illus-
trates the power of magnetic influences upon our
media, and the necessity of keeping the physical system in a state of health, and the mind well balanced
with hopeful feelings, aspirations, and happy associations, as sure guards against temptation. It shows,

too, the cunning of obsessing spirits in times of need and peril, like the one who came to Jesus in the wilderness, suggesting that he make use of his spiritual gifts in administering to his physical needs, even though his parental angels had promised protection through all his ministry.

Whilst lecturing in an Eastern city, the gentleman medium of whom we speak became acquainted with a young man who was proud, spiritual, poor, and disposed to learn. Seeing him attired in clothes scarcely decent to appear in meeting, he said:

"Would to God that I had the means to put that young man in a position to rise in the world. The now departed of other years helped me; I must help others. It is blessed to give. But my family *must* have my first attention."

Then the spirit whispered:

"Does not humanity constitute one family?"

Giving the worthy young man some valuable books suited to his needs, he bade him good cheer with words of sympathy. Soon after, returning in a steamer from a distant city where he lectured, a friend met him in a street. The poor fellow was pale and dejected.

"Why, brother, where have you been," he asked, "that you look so haggard and woe-begone? Are you sick?"

"No," was the reply, "not sick, but I had no sleep last night on board a crowded steamer."

"Reduced so much in one night? why, you droop like wilted grass. Did you not get well paid?"

" Got enough to cover expenses to and from. Why are you so inquisitive?"

At length it was wormed out of him—the history of that wild night on the crowded steamer. To no mortal had he lisped it, but " seeing you will know all about me," he added, " and will never betray my confidence, I must out with it. I have been in a gambling saloon!"

Strange as it may seem, there is an angel's hand in all this, and the moral is very beautiful.

On board the steamer were about thirteen hundred passengers; not a stateroom, nor berth, nor chair, could be procured. He therefore wandered round from place to place—a time when one is attracted by every trivial incident, a time of negation — and unconsciously went down into the lower cabin, when he heard voices laughing and shouting at one end of the boat. Elbowing his way through the motley crowd, a looker on, he at length found a band of gamblers seated round a table, one man using the cards with his confederates, who assumed to be his enemies and opposers, engaged in betting, each of whom put down a hundred dollars. The medium noticed a black spot on a certain card, and said to his nearest neighbor:

" They can see the mark on that card; don't fool away your money so!"

Turning round to him with an appearance of feeling insulted, the gambler said, with a design of provoking an adventure:

" I know my own business, sir. I don't care a damn—got my pocket full of rocks."

Then a fine-dressed gentleman stepped up to him with the air of an indifferent adviser, and suggestively said:

"Suppose you put down a hundred dollars; you will get it. I have won four hundred dollars to-night; as long as the money is going, you might as well have some of it as myself. Put down a hundred dollars."

"Why, I never gambled in my life," said he, quite dreamily.

"'Tis n't gambling—only put money in the pocket and say nothing. Why, you have a beautiful cross (taking it patronizingly in his fingers), you can give your money to some benevolent institution — some orphan asylum—and do good by it—come!"

The bait was alluring. At that moment the thought of that young man flashed on his mind in hopeful vision.

"Yes, I can get him a suit of clothes and make him happy. I will do good with the money which these gamblers otherwise will use in debauchery."

Whilst he thus was cogitating, as oblivious to himself as a star in a midnight cloud, a long-nosed Jew said loudly to a gambler:

"Don't put down any more; you are an old fool! you will lose all you have."

To which the gambler retorted, "Damn you, go away. I know my business."

This answer had the desired effect.

"The young man in Boston! Oh, can I not help him?" said he in silent revery. Then he hesitated— "is this not gambling? Oh, the poor young man!"

He was exhausted, had nothing to eat, negative, psychologized, obsessed, bewildered, entranced by spirits on a low plane, wrapped in their subtle influence till almost unconscious.

The well-dressed gentleman, noticing the mental vibration, pursued his advantage:

"These devils, whose life I detest, will spend their money in drink; you will do good with it."

And our medium thought then how many he could thus bless. The temptation gained, the tempter gloated, the decision was made—"I'll do it!" was his secret resolution.

As he took out his money his conscience smote to the quick, and whispered, "Beware of gambling!" but sympathy for that young man triumphed. "I will snatch the money from these demons; why, they all make money; I'll get—and—*do*—GOOD!" and planked down a hundred dollar bill! Another man covered it with a hundred dollars. Three cards lay side by side as before, and one of these the lucky spotted card that won every time, when the chief gambler said:

"Sir, which will you have?"

The medium put his hand on the spotted card; the man turned it over—it was not *the* card!

"You've lost," said the arch gambler, with a business-like coolness; "who planks next?"

The well-dressed gentleman, as if consoling the medium, touched his arm, saying, "Try it again; you will win the next time; I'll go you halves."

He immediately left the place, and passed up to the

upper cabin and breathed a purer air, when he felt a different inspiration, followed by remorse, and exclaimed aloud, " Who can tell who are friends? What is life? O God, save me! O angels, come to me!"

" Who are friends?" softly said a spirit guide, "what is life? O, my brother, my brother!"

Then he was folded in calm reflection, as if a hand of safety held his, and a holy impression, never to be forgotten, rested on his mind, the dark cloud now transfiguring him:

" You have learned a lesson at a dear cost; you can speak of gambling as never before. You will never be off your guard again with such company. You perceive that when you enter a certain state of magnetism you can be influenced by spirits of a corresponding character. Never be negative with such associates. Watch! go forth! you are wiser—gird on the sword of reform again—wiser and better!"

> " It never pays to wreck the health
>   In drudging after gain,
>   And he is sold who thinks that gold
>   Is cheaply bought with pain.
>
>   The good and pure alone are sure
>   To bring prolonged success,
>   While what is right in Heaven's sight
>   Is always sure to bless."

11

CHAPTER VII

AMONG the primal causes of obsession is the inculcation of low and groveling sentiment. If, as has been shown, every letter we write, every article of clothing we wear, and, in fact, everything we touch, contains the psychological imprint of our personal magnetism, how much more potent must be the thought or idea of subtle mind from its brainial battery, directly impressing mere negatives who reverence such teachers as heaven-appointed oracles! Popes, priests, and ministers of every sect have been held in esteem for their religious office; and when these improve their opportunity to retain social power, how easy it is to mold the moral and spiritual character of the masses! Were these sustaining a natural and inspirational relation with the masses, instructing them in the laws of their being rather than book knowledge, ever with a view to progressive improvement in every possible manner, what an incalculable amount of good could they accomplish! But the facts are potent that, as a general rule, they build their churches upon mere theory, organize their sects upon fossilized dogmas, and are therefore ancient in make-up of character, with magnetic forces of the same grade, chained and chaining, dead and deadening, "blind leaders of the blind," even in the great blaze of scientific light burning all around them. Sentiment is a molder of mind, and if unnatural and dismal, it drags down to its own plane of horrors whatever it can grasp. Like begets like; this is a law of life in all its multiform uses. The theology of a personal devil, of an implacable deity, of a bloody atonement to appease his wrath and satisfy divine justice, and of a hell of endless torments, being dark and frightful ideals, and appealing only to low considerations, have produced negative states of moral character, inductive to infestuous influences from corresponding associations, both in the human and spirit worlds. By these theological implements have the priests transformed our naturally beautiful world into Hadean serfdoms, debased the religious nature of man, and perverted the passions to exhale a moral malaria from the earth to the immortal spheres. A depraved idea of our humanity is the very mother of sin itself.

A few quotations from some theological authors will suffice to show how damning must have been the moral influences of such sentiments still lingering in the shadows of a night that is slowly paling into morning of a brighter day:

" Every sin, both original and eternal, being a transgression of the righteous law of God, and contrary thereunto, doth in its own nature bring guilt upon the sinner, whereby he is bound over to the wrath of God, and curse of the law, and so made subject to death, with miseries spiritual, temporal, and eternal."—
Westminster Confession.

Rev. Thomas Boston, in his " Four-fold State," informs us that:

" The godly wife shall applaud the justice of the judge in the condemnation of her *ungodly husband*. The godly husband shall say *amen!* to the damnation of her who lay in his bosom! The godly parent shall say *halleluiah!* at the passing of the sentence of their ungodly child. And the godly child shall from the heart approve the *damnation* of his wicked parents who begot him, and the mother who bore him."— p. 336.

Calvin, speaking of the mortal condition of infants, and the effects of hereditary depravity, employs the following language:

" It is hereditary depravity and corruption of our nature, diffused through all parts of the soul, which in the first place, exposes us to the wrath of God," etc. (Institutes ii: 1–8.) Of infants, he says: "They bring their condemnation with them from their mother's womb, being liable to punishment not for the sins of another, but for their own. For, although they have not yet produced the fruits of their iniquity, yet they have the seed enclosed in themselves; nay, their whole nature is, as it were, a seed of sin; therefore it cannot but be odious and abominable to God. Whence it follows that it (the infant's corrupt nature) is properly considered sin before God, because there could not be liability to punishment without sin."—*Institutes* ii: 1–8.

Calvin, in his Theological Tracts, addresses Sebastian Castalio, for teaching that all laws, human and divine, condemn a man *after* and because of transgression, in the following words:

" You deny that it is just in God to damn any one, unless on account of transgression. Persons innumerable are taken out of life while yet infants. Put forth now your virulence against God who *precipitates into eternal death harmless infants, (innoxious fœtus) torn from their mothers' breasts.* He who will not detest this blasphemy [of yours] when it is only exposed, may curse me at his will. For it cannot be demanded that I should be safe and free from the abuse of those who do not spare God."—*Tract Theology.—Columniæ Nebulonis, etc., Art.* 14.

Parson Wiggleworth, we think it was, a New England clergyman, taught this:

> " Have faith the same
> With endless shame
> For all the human race,
> For Hell is crammed
> With infants, damned
> Without a day of grace."

In the "Practical Sermons" of Edwards, occurs this passage:

" The saints in glory will be far more sensible how dreadful the wrath of God is, and will better understand how terrible the sufferings of the damned are, yet this will be no occasion of grief to them, but rejoicing. They will not be sorry for the damned; it will cause no uneasiness or dissatisfaction to them, but on the contrary, when they see this sight, it will

occasion rejoicing, and excite them to joyful praises."
Watts, in his hymns, further dilates upon the subject:

> " A point of time, a moment's space,
>   Removes me to that heavenly place,
>   Or shuts me up in hell."
> " But vengeance and damnation lies
>   On rebels who refuse the grace;
>   Who God's Eternal Son despise,
>   The hottest hell shall be their place."

These gems of Evangelism were formerly sung in
churches, and termed "making melody in the heart
to God."

The Rev. Thomas Vincent, a Calvanistic clergyman
of the Seventeenth century, indulges in the following
strain:

"This will fill them (the saints) with astonishing
admiration and wondering joy, when they see some
of their near relatives going to hell; their fathers, their
mothers, their children, their husbands, their wives,
their intimate friends and companions, while they
themselves are saved! * * * Those affections they
now have for relatives *out* of Christ will *cease;* and
they will not have the *least trouble* to see them sen-
tenced to *hell*, and thrust into the *fiery furnace!* "

The American Reform Tract and Book Society, of
Cincinnati, published a few years since the following
from the Rev. James Smith:

"The fire of hell is such that multitudes of tears
will not quench it, and length of time will not burn it
out. 'The wrath of God abideth' on the rejecter of
Christ." (*John* iii: 36.)

"Oh, eternity! eternity! Who can fathom it? Mariners have their plummet to measure the depths of the sea; but what line or plummet shall we use to fathom the depth of eternity? The breath of the Lord kindles the flames of the pit (*Isaiah* xxx: 33), and where shall we find waters to quench those flames? OH, ETERNITY! If all the body of the earth and the sea were turned to sand, and all the space up to the starry heaven were nothing but sand, and if a little bird should come once every thousand years and take away in her bill but a single grain from all that heap of sand, what numberless years and ages must be spent before the whole of that vast quantity would be carried away. Yet if even at the end of all that time the sinner might come out of hell, there would be some hope. But that word FOREVER breaks the heart. 'The smoke of their torment ascendeth up for ever and ever.'"

Nothing is plainer in psychological law than that selfish and dismal sentiment generates fear in the mind of the recipient, and this in turn a negative condition of moral character on the animal plane, so transporting the hells of theology to our fair world. The social ruin of all this cannot abate until more natural and happy views of life and duty are mutually entertained by the inhabitants of both worlds.

We would not detract one iota from the virtue of a single individual, and would ever reckon in the balances of justice the age in which live the representatives of religious thought, and so be large in credit of charity;

but we cannot sincerely apologize for the dogmas they
inculcated when the better part of human nature
revolts with disgust and horror, more especially so
with the educated.   Bitter must be the weeping of the
clergy who, in the spirit life, discover their doctrines
have peopled it with dark and debased specimens of
citizens there, here molded in falsehoods.   The greater
the culpability to preserve these debasing dogmas in
this age of scientific light, when every sensible mind
scorns them as irrational and licentious in their effects
both upon this world and the next.   We once conversed
with a dark, unhappy spirit, through Mr. Burns, of
Coldwater, Michigan—a reliable man.   On inquiry we
learned the spirit had in earth-life preached the doctrine of the atonement, a personal devil, and an endless
hell.   He averred with sorrowful regret that such
teaching had cast him into outer darkness.

THE EVANGELICAL ALLIANCE.

The thinkers and reformers were looking for a
" church departure," but to the world's staggering disappointment, the Evangelical Alliance, held in New
York, October, 1873, represented by Protestants,
has again planted itself squarely on the old basis,
rebuilding and patching up the same theological peni-
tentiary.   Here is the platform:

1. The divine inspiration, authority, and *sufficiency*
of the Holy Scriptures.

2. Right and duty of private judgment in their
interpretation.

3. The Unity and Trinity of the Godhead.

4. The *utter* depravity of human nature in consequence of the *fall*.

5. Justification by faith.

6. The influence of the Holy Spirit

7. The immortality of the soul.

8. The resurrection of the body.

9. The final judgment.

10. The divine institution of the Christian ministry.

Seers see in this perpetuation of dismal dogmas and priestly power, drifting steadily to a union of church and state, a dark hour for American liberty, over which angels are prophetically weeping.

With what loathing do the city people shun the water in the tanks and sewers. All the scum of the town flows in there—the overflowings of filthy cellars, the soakings of the stables, the drainage of blocks in every direction. The inhabitants know it is full of pestilence and deadness; so, far off they go to the mountain streams of liquid crystal. They bridge an aqueduct thither, and draw it thence over vales, under hills, and through the forests, into the thirsty city, where it branches off into thousands of little pipes— a refreshing unity in diversity—and leaps up with laughter in the public walks, bedewing the gardens, washing the streets, rejoicing the blameless beasts, purifying and blessing every house, and thousands are glad as the Hebrews when Moses smote the rock of Horeb. How long shall we drink of the slough of ages? "The whole head is faint, and the whole heart

sick." Is there no escape from sectarian prisons, whose
air is dead and poisonous, to the mountains of free
thought? Oh, the panting and thirsting! In the *deserts*
of popular theology souls are perishing! The promised oasis of the fashionable church is but the delusive
mirage of sin! Let us hasten to the Carmels and Oli-
vets of inspiration, and find the many flowing waters
of the river of life.

CONFOUNDING OF VIRTUE AND VICE.

The responsibility of stoical moralists of to-day is
even greater than that of the clergy, when, under a
superior light, they make chaos of virtue and vice, and
so blind the negative people with seductive meta-
physics, forcing their own intellects to veil their own
follies under seeming reason.

"It is possible," said Paracelsus, "that my spirit,
without the help of the body, and through a fiery will
alone, can wound others. It is also possible that I can
bring the spirit of my adversary into an image, and
then double him up to his displeasure. Will is a great
point in the art of medicine. Man can hang disease
on man and beast through curses. * * * Every
imagination of man proceeds from the centre of his
being. This is the sun of the microcosm; and out of
the microcosm flows the imagination into the great
world. Thus the imagination of man is a seed which
becomes materialized into the outer. * * * The
imagination of another may be able to kill me. Imagination springing out of pleasure and desire usually

acts in concert with the will power; therefore envy and hatred follow; for desire is followed by the deed. No armor protects against magical influences, for they injure the inward spirit of life."

The heart speaks though the lips belie; and true it is, " He that soweth to the flesh shall of the flesh reap corruption."

Against such applies the apostolic injunction: " For we wrestle not against flesh and blood, but against principalities, against powers, against the rulers of the darkness of this world, against spiritual wickedness [wicked spirits] in high places."—*Ephesians* vi: 12.

To point out errors in the social fabric without substituting something better; to mingle so much vinegar with the milk of philanthropy as to make it utterly distasteful to the multitude, is, to say the most, but slightly benefiting humanity. The " waster should be the builder, too," says Whittier, and Carlyle insists that reformers should go forth with " hammers for building, as well as torches for burning." Deeply interested in every genuine reform of the age, in everything that benefits and spiritualizes the great brotherhood of races, the voices of Spiritualists should ever go forth, " Repent, repent ye, for the kingdom of heaven is at hand." And is it not an hour for retrenchment? A magnetic gluttony, and then a starvation, is poor economy. A great sensation, and then a " burnt district," is a chaotic policy. The words of the Nazarene are applicable to us at this stage of our growth, when all around obsessing influences madden and fever even to the spirit world: "Behold, I give you power to tread on serpents and scorpions, and over all the power of the enemy; and nothing shall by any means hurt you. Notwithstanding, in this rejoice not, that the spirits are subject unto you; but rather rejoice because your names are written in heaven."

Joel Tiffany, who was and is a Spiritualist as well as a logician and moral philosopher, says: "There are those who have lost their higher aspirations; who have ceased to make the proper distinctions between virtue and vice, between the pure and the impure impulses of the soul; who have become, and are becoming, victims of a sensual philosophy. * * * No man will ever defend or excuse the practice of any vice or crime from an inward approbation; nor will he seek to lessen the estimated difference between virtue and vice, justice or crime, unless he wishes to take advantage thereof. The intemperate drinker seeks to justify drinking; the libertine apologizes for sensuality; and the oppressor seeks to excuse his oppression; and when we hear any one judging favorably of any practice, we are justified in judging him by his judgment. * * * This kind of Spiritualism has led its advocates generally to fall into the too common error of trying to redeem the world without first redeeming themselves.

"It has revealed the faults of others, but not their own. They have seen the mote in their neighbor's eye, but not the beam in their own. They tell of the redemptive power of such Spiritualism, while they remain unredeemed by it. If its influence upon the

world to overcome selfishness, appetite, passion, and
lust shall be no greater than it has been upon themselves, the world will not be redeemed; the millenium
will be postponed until the coming of some other
Messiah."

We also commend to their contemplation the wise
saying of Buddha: "The three poisons, covetousness,
anger and delusion, which rage within the heart, and
the five obscurities, envy, passion, sloth, vaccillation
and unbelief, which embrace it, effectually prevent one
from obtaining supreme reason. But once get rid of
the pollution of the heart, and then we perceive the
spiritual portions of ourselves, which we have had
from the first, although involved in the net of life and
death; gladly, then, we mount the paradise of all the
Bhoods, where reason and virtue continually abide."
And of Zoroaster: "Every man who is pure in
thought, words, and actions, will go to the celestial
regions. Every man who is evil in thought, word, or
actions, will go to a place of punishment." And of
the Nazarene: "By thy words thou shalt be justified,
and by thy words thou shalt be condemned."

WHAT SHALL WE DO TO BE SAVED?

Says Dr. R. T. Trall: "No truth in philosophy is
better established than the fact that bodily purity and
true morality hold intimate and reciprocal relations.
Try if you can, reader, to entertain the idea of a glut-
tonous eater, a wine-bibber, or a tobacco-user, in
connection with holiness of heart. There is something

unnatural, revolting, repulsive, in the association.
Just as the bodily appetences and the outward senses
are depraved, does the inner man, the moral nature,
become gross. The pure spirit will not, cannot, dwell
in a filthy tenement. There is a natural correspond-
ence between material and spiritual things, so that the
quality of one denotes the character of the other."

Measure another court of your customary sin.
Only one page of to-day's horrors — only a small percentage of child-murdering come to light; but a true
registry is kept — the "book of life" contains fearful
records over which angels weep. Look with clairvoyant
eyes into the rivers, and lakes, and sewers, and privies,
and scan the partially developed forms, rotting to skele-
tons, of hundreds of infants. Others are consumed
in fires, devoured by starving city dogs, or buried
secretly under midnight darkness, uncoffined and
unknelled.

Oh, fathers! forcing women to this awful crime by
social oppressions to earn a living by prostitution —
prostitution of your own wives and daughters, too —
what is that blot upon your soul, whereon not a
repentant tear has yet fallen? Read, read the ominous
blot — *murder!* Alas, where shall we turn, whence
shall we fly, to find integrity? Who can lift up his
hands and say, "God, I thank thee, I am not as other
men are?" Who, perceiving there is no virtue where
lust has cast but a single stain upon the heart, or
fœticide has engraved its dreaded brand of "*murderer*" upon the memory, can refrain from smiting

his breast in deep sorrow, saying, "God be merciful to me a sinner?"

What of the children who, despite poisonous drugs, escape death in the fœtus, whose fathers, shamed and confused at the mishap of conception, demand abortion to secure speedier opportunities for married adultery; whose mothers, recoiling before the sorrows of child-birth and the prospects of newly added cares at home, despairingly resolve upon abortion, thus stamping forever upon the coming child the intent of suicide — what of such children? Are they healthy, orderly, spiritual, beautiful, happy? Sad truth! the world is peopling with unwelcome children! children with dwarfed and idiotic spiritualities, discordant affections, brutalized passions, sinking humanity lower and lower to a plane of demoniac incarnation.

Notice the effect of this murdering of the innocents upon the mothers. Behold their pale, sallow faces, their hectic cheeks, their feeble step, their soul-sorrow, secretly kept but plainly visible in every lineament of the countenance, revealing as on a dial plate the sad workings of the heart. Are they fallen — fallen? If the babe escapes the attempt at abortion, the mother loves it — loves the babe of accident — weeps bitterly if a little grave hides it from sight. Thus sacred is human nature, even when poisoned at the fountains of life! Does not all this prove how easy is human regeneration, and how divine will be our homes under the law of a wisely directed love?

Abortion, like the death angel of Egypt, sprinkles

blood upon the lintels of nearly every house. Even when love is pure and not a passion is unholy, many a married pair, whose wisdom as yet demands no child, falls a prey to the scourge. They mean no harm. It was an accident; but does nature credit for the accident? Will the world know it? Heaven knows it, trembling victim of the serpent!

Is conscience undisturbed? Ask the wife's pale lips, the genital weakness, the alarm of the loving husband. Their love may be constant; nearer may they cling to each other, as wounded birds in one nest, as if mutual sympathy might palliate for this outrage upon nature. How many degrees does the dial of life discount? Ask the gravestones that say with silent tenderness, as if the very marble would weep — aged twenty! aged twenty-five! aged thirty! Oh, they are young wives! All such concussions of body jar not only the spiritual organism, but tremble out upon the magnetic atmosphere, there picturing *murder*, seen and felt in spirit life.

CONCEPTIVE IMMORTALITY.

To the dark and frightful picture of our sensual life we would add another figure, central in it, for all men and women to stare at, that the responsibilities of passional excesses and obsessional pollutions reach on to the coming world! Conception is immortal life in embryo. All the murdered buds will yet be laid at our feet! The awful consequences of these acts will be realized in spirit agony as they were in the physical, when nature was so outraged! We would fain hide from the picture, but cannot; it stares us in the face everywhere. Great God! whose justice never sleeps — angels! whose hearts are " touched with the feeling of our infirmity," is there no reprieve, no deliverance from this "abomination of desolation " in our social life? Fathers and mothers! young men and maidens! what is the handwriting of heaven, traced in blood? " Repent! *repent!* by adaptable relations of life with chastity of habits.

SOCIAL DISPARITIES.

If the central love of two persons are on diverse spheral planes, the one spiritual and the other sensual, they instinctively repel. Either the spiritual must descend to the sensual, and there be buried, or else the sensual must ascend to the spiritual regenerated, ere there can be harmony between the two. Just here lies the secret of our social troubles. The spiritual influx from the angel world has blossomed out some souls as flowers in summer; the organically spiritual have responded and passed to a higher plane of life. These love more, love deeper, love purer, as angels do, and hence require more spiritual magnetism to supply the soul. Having thus eaten, so to speak, of the tree of life in Eden, to descend to a merely animal life, to live for self, to gratify the " lusts of the flesh," is the starvation and damnation of hell. Either the sensual mate must be regenerated and spiritualized, or dissolution of soul-copartnership must ensue. " What

12

concord hath Christ with Belial?" The animal plane, when unguided by celestial wisdom, preys upon its victim — is pleased most when the sweet and beautiful of heaven becomes the servant of its lust. To descend here, after the soul "has passed from this death unto life," is an unpardonable sin. The voice of the angel is, "Come up hither!" Come where every faculty and function is no longer a dead Golgotha, but a mount of transfiguration, where all loves are free, natural and holy.

CORRELATION OF PHYSICAL AND SPIRITUAL FORCES.

Principles are primal springs of being, the *esse* of things. Laws are but their modes of action. Forms are results of both — the crystals of spirit, the life mirror that reflects the unseen to the seen. In principles are laid our individuality, expressing an identity by embodiment ever recognizable. Life chemistries call it out. It seems to have been the aim of the Infinite through various mediations, and such experiences as life-epics, lyrics, tragedies and comedies, substances and shadows, pointed thorns and radiant rose-leaves, to educate or help each mortal to become self-poised and harmonial. The most perfect figure is a sphere, each part being equally distant from the centre; and still every sphere is an individuality, though neither angular nor irregular. So in the divine symmetry of the angel, no one faculty or quality puts out, obtaining undue position or action over the others, for each has its place, function and mission with reference to the whole. Thus angels and archangels, crowned with wisdom and love, are poised and counterpoised, excelling in all things.

If a man's ruling love is lust of appetite, it takes form in a putrid face, bleared eyes, calloused brain, guttural voice, and a beastly organism generally. If it is lust for wealth, his every faculty and sense, his mouth, eye, ear, nose, lip, beard, step, gesture, are so many "stocks in trade." If it is for literature, he has an intellectual head, intellectual manners, intellectual coat, intellectual boots, intellectual starch in his very collar. By this law of love we are molded, as the potter molds the clay.

Nor is there a chance for deception before the inspecting angels. "They know at once the whole man, perceiving by the tone of his voice the affection that reigns in his thought; and by his behavior or form of action the love that rules in his will. They have a clear perception of such things, however a man may strive to conceal his true character under an appearance of religion and morality."

The spirit is ever building its own house, beautiful or deformed, as its instinct is, both here and hereafter. No doubt there are modifying forces at work to prevent a true expression. Outward circumstances check our best effort. The common misfortunes of life sometimes limn the face and form into ugly visages. But remember such transfiguring influences must work first upon the spirit where all causation lies, changing there its nature to organize a corresponding physical contour. Surroundings are secondary in the molding of life and character. They may retard or impede the process of structure; yet the spirit is the ever-busy artist, carving for itself from the best material it can get to make for itself a "suitable habitation and a name." As spiritual beings we are transformed into the likeness of those virtues for which we have an admiration.

"There is no sculpture like the mind," says the *Phrenological Journal.* "The man who thinks, reads, meditates aright, has intelligence in his features, stamped on his brow, and gleaming in his eye. There is nothing that so refines and ennobles face and mein as the constant presence of great thoughts, a high determination, a virtuous principle, an unquenchable enthusiasm. But more powerful still than any of these, as a beautifier of the person, is the overmastering purpose and pervading disposition of impartial kindness in the heart, a universal benevolence, and desire to make others happy. The soul that is full of pure and generous affections, fashions the features into its own angelic likeness, as the rose, by inherent impulse, grows in grace and blossoms into a loveliness which art cannot equal."

CHAPTER VIII.

"SET THINE HOUSE IN ORDER."

THE POWER of *exorcising*, or casting out evil spirits, varies according to educational notions and creedal practices. The Catholic Church, from time immemorial, basing its authority upon Apostolic custom, has made use of consecrated water sprinkled upon the obsessed, and certain established rites and prayers, with the sign of the cross. Similar magical enchantments were used, particularly by St. Gregory the Great, St. Epiphanius, St. Jerome, St. Hilarion, Theodoret, Palladius, and others.

In *La Messenger*, of Leige, for October, 1873 (translated by G. L. Ditson, M. D., for the *Banner of Light*), is the following, speaking of Layard's discoveries at Nineveh: "This primitive Spiritualism had a recognized existence (in Assyria); a considerable portion of the religious rites of the people of this country consisted of invocations, and above all, of sacred words, to chase away evil spirits, to whom were attributed a large part of human ills. One published tablet contained a series of prayers or of sacramental words, serving to preserve a woman *enciente* and the nurse from evils that come to afflict. * * * The words used in the middle ages by the exorcists, ' *Va-*

t-en, va-t-en, mauvais, mauvais,' are purely and simply
a reproduction *textuelle* of the words pronounced by
the magi of the Chaldeans four to six thousand years
ago: *Xilka, xilka, besa, besa.* These Assyrian words,
transmitted from generation to generation, have always
been regarded as having a mysterious and sovereign
power to shield one from the spirit of the 'clouds,' or
of 'darkness.' "

Exorcists are intellectually positive. As to the mere
method of casting out, moral qualities are not essential. But it does so depend where the subject is to be
magnetically insulated against a return of the same or
similar obsessions. An immoral man with a powerful
will can drive out a spirit; but the mental battery of
the subject is only thus changed for a new class of
obsessing influences, perhaps more entangling than
before. The Nazarene, knowing this fact, thus
describes the magnetic exchange from one obsession
to another, showing the absolute necessity of moral
ability to produce a thorough dispossession: "When
the unclean spirit is gone out of a man, he walketh
through dry places, seeking rest; and finding none, he
saith, I will return unto my house whence I came out.
And when he cometh, he findeth it swept and gar-
nished. Then goeth he, and taketh with him seven
other spirits more wicked than himself, and they enter
in and dwell there; and the last state of that man is
worse than the first."

BOY RECLAIMED FROM AN EVIL SPIRIT.

In the life of Apollonius, of Tyana, by Philostra-

tus, we have this singular account: " In the midst of a
conversation between Apollonius and some wise men,
a messenger arrived, introducing to these sages some
people from India. Among them was a woman who
came to intercede for her son, a youth of about sixteen
years of age, who for the last two years was possessed
of a lying, wicked demon. One of the sages asked on
what grounds she said this. 'Because,' replied she,
'a demon has fallen in love with him for his beauty,
who suffers him not to enjoy any freedom of will, nor
go to school, nor shoot his bow, nor even stay at home,
but drags him abroad into lonely and desert places.
Besides,' said she, 'he no longer retains his natural
voice, but speaks like a man, and sees objects with eyes
very different from his own. This is the cause why I
weep and tear my bosom, and endeavor all I can to
have him restored to his right mind; but alas! he
knows me not. At the same time, I must tell you that
when once I made up my mind to come to you, which
is now more than a year, the demon confessed by the
mouth of my boy as his interpreter, who he is. He
avowed himself to be the ghost of a man who had
fallen long ago in battle, and who had been extremely
fond of his wife; but that when he understood she had
violated his marriage bed, and wedded another man
only three days after his death, his love for the sex
turned to hatred, and all his affections passed to this
boy. At last the demon promised, on the condition
of my making no complaint to you, that he would do
my son much good. I suffered myself to be tempted

by his promises; but he has now long deceived me, and has got possession of my house, which he keeps without one sentiment of truth or honor.' Here one of the sages asked if the boy was at hand. His mother said he was not, for the demon did all he could to prevent his coming; for precipices dire, and death itself were held out by way of threats should I bring him before your tribunal. 'Take courage, woman,' said the wise man, 'for as soon as he has read this letter he will harm you not;' and with these words he took one from his bosom and gave it to the woman, which was written to the spectre, containing many things, enough not only to alarm, but terrify him. And he left."

CURANTA SIMILIBUS — INSANITIES.

Apollonius, possessing great power even over the animal creation, on his way through Tarsus found a man who had been bitten thirty days before by a mad dog, and who was then running on all fours, barking and howling. Having obtained a description of the dog, he said, looking forth clairvoyantly: "He is now standing near the fountain, wishing to drink. Go bring him hither; you have only to say that I want him." He then went on to explain the law of *curanta similibus*, and cited the case of Telephus, who was cured by the spear that wounded him. "When the dog was brought he patted him, and induced him to lick the place where he had been bitten; whereupon the young man was restored to his right mind."

Says Rev. William R. Alger, in a lecture: " The fundamental phenomena of insanity are equally exhibited in delirium tremens, the exaltations and hallucinations of fevers, also in persons under the influence of opium or hashish; but in these exhibitions the force of the phenomena is brief, the termination is foreseen, and the cause is understood; therefore the mystic horror and dread are wanting. And yet insanity itself, in its worst phases, is not any more a diabolical chaos than the phenomena manifested under these other conditions; it is equally with the various departments and experiences of sanity and health, under the domain of law, following regular sequences of cause and effect, having a beginning and end appropriate to itself, and running through its normal course, which is generally understood by those who are experts in the matter. It is all covered with the lines of order and law — the symmetrical and systematic regularity and harmony which is the leading characteristic of all the workings of God in Nature."

The curative agencies vary according to conditions; and chief among them, as the constantly working force, is psychic pathology, with the appliances of neatness, order, purity, amusement, and physiological regularity. As yet the psychological is the least employed, being the least understood as a remedial agent.

Dr. John A. Weise, quoting from a work of Dr. Grath Wilkinson, on " A Proposal to Treat Lunacy by Spiritualism," says: " Lunacy is essentially a mental

13

derangement.   Why is it not logical to infer that the
mental aura has attracted and harbors correspondingly
affinitive spirits, whose sport the lunatic becomes?   In
our historical survey we have seen that all nations
believed in and acted upon this doctrine; that the
wisest and best of our race entertained this belief in
some form or other.   Religions, creeds, sects, theories
and opinions are based upon it.   Modern Spiritualism
is trying to prove it by induction, and put it on a
scientific and practical basis."

About A. D. 300, the treatment of lunacy is
mentioned in the sanitary laws enacted at Rome.
According to Posidonius, nervous and mental diseases
are owing to the disturbance of the spirit or soul
organs.   Demons, talismans and exorcism were used
to cure them.

"The Essæans, a certain order of learned Jews in
Egypt, imbued with Zoroastrian, Pythagorean, Jewish
and Christian ideas, taught that all diseases, especially
insanity, could be cured through the influence of a
contemplative life, and the agency of angels."

Professor Ferrier, of England, experimenting on the
brains of animals by electricity, and thereby producing
astonishing effects, was led to apply the electrodes on
the various organs of the human brain by an exterior
manipulation, and was enabled to materially change
the character of the people who came to him as
patients.   Says a London correspondent: "His power
is especially marked in cases of depraved alimentive-
ness — especially in dipsomania, the alcoholic thirst.

By the application of electricity to that portion of the brain which comprehends the alimentive faculties, and attends to eating and drinking, the diseased longing is made to cease; and, by a course of continued application the drunkard's depraved appetite is not only cured, but he acquires an intense aversion to all kinds of alcoholic stimulus. People of extreme irritability, of great combativeness and destructiveness are soothed by the application of electricity, so that the irritability disappears and they become amiable and agreeable companions. Women who are scolds, and men who are fierce and brutal in temperament; persons who are afflicted with melancholia, or excessive caution, or extreme nervousness, are all susceptible of cure under these strange methods.

"But the most surprising effect of electricity upon the brain is in regard to sleep. As physiologists are aware, no part of the human system sleeps except the brain. During our nightly repose the blood circulates, the stomach digests, the liver and kidneys secrete their humors, and all the functions of the body continue in operation — not so actively, perhaps, as when we are awake, but certainly with very little perceptible difference. The only part of the human economy, then, in which any change appears to be effected in sleep is the brain and nervous system, which, in their normal condition, require varying periods of repose. But the professor, according to his friends, has discovered that the time of sleep may be reduced to a minimum; that one or two hours will be amply sufficient hereafter when this system has been applied to the human race, and that this enormous gain can be made without affecting the integrity of the nervous system or limiting the duration of life."

Evidently here is a magnetic law of cure, practical in curing obsessed insanities. It is the opinion of the most eminent psychologists that three-quarters of the insane are obsessed, and, as experiments in various ways demonstrate, that the same force which depolarized their brainial action by unadaptable magnetism, can be successfully used in cure. This has been done in isolated cases, and why not on a more extensive scale in our asylums? Nothing is more important for superintendents and physicians to investigate. A historian tells us that a wild boy found in the forest of Aiden, in 1563, "saved the sheep from devouring wolves by rubbing his spittle on them. He had been brought up by a she wolf."

The ancient Egyptians adopted a psychical method of cure, worthy of our imitation. "At both extremities of Egypt were temples dedicated to Saturn, to which melancholics and obsessed persons resorted in great numbers. In these abodes, surrounded by shady groves and beautiful gardens, varieties of games and recreations were established for the amusement of the mind and the invigoration of the body, while the imagination was impressed with the finest productions of the sculptor and painter. * * * Music, love, employment, exercising the memory, and fixing the attention, were also among the remedies."

Pythagoras and Asclepiades introduced a similar cure in Greece.

CHRISTIAN EXORCISM.

Justin Martyr, in his Apology, declares that the Christians of his time "healed in every part of the world, and dispossessed evil spirits" in the name of Jesus.

Tertulian, himself obsessed, taught the doctrine of evil influences, as well as good. The inspiration that moved him was most ferocious. He enjoined the most malignant treatment against the rival media of unchristian sects.

Apollinaris, a Ravennian Bishop of note, accompanying the Apostle Peter to Rome, and preaching on the eastern coast of Italy, is said to have silenced the oracles of Roman temples, and "caused deceiving spirits to depart therefrom." Having a masterly psychological power, he "cast out demons and converted vast multitudes to the principles of Jesus." Other Christian fathers, and among them Origen, believed that by prayer and reading of sacred writings "demons could be cast out and numberless evils averted."

"Theological opinion has nowhere undergone such strange mutations as in New England. There Unitarianism acquired its firmest seat, and there Spiritualism has won its chief triumphs. A curious instance of the action of these two heresies (shall we say?) is before us in an article entitled 'The Perfection of Jesus,' in *Old and New*, a Boston monthly magazine, written by the Rev. J. F. Clarke, a distinguished Unitarian preacher. 'As regards Demoniacal Possession,' writes Mr. Clarke, 'I think that Jesus believed in it, and that he spoke to the evil spirits as though they would hear him. A few years ago I thought that he shared a popular error in this, which our century had outgrown. But within a few years I have been led to believe in the reality of Demoniacal Possession. I have myself known personally, or by credible testimony, of at least half a dozen instances of persons who, after having allowed themselves to become spiritual mediums, seem at last to have been taken possession of by a low and unclean order of spirits. And the best way of rescuing them, when they were too far gone to help themselves, was to have some other person possessing greater spiritual force to do what Jesus did, namely, *order the spirit to go away.* I believe that in certain places and periods the nervous condition of men is such that the lower order of ghosts may get control over them, and that when Jesus came, it was just such a time and place as this.'"—*New Londoner.*

SUPERSTITIOUS METHODS.

People, in their superstitions, try to cast out by the Bible, or in the name of Jesus Christ. Negative spirits so educated, may yield; but the method is a farce. In the name of Mahomet, or wise Apollonius, is just as available if the magnetic *will* is equally potent. The name to conjure by is an old whim of the church. Again, people fancy they can guard against evil influences — forgetful that this is a sign the magnet so drawing is in themselves — by hugging the Bible, rigid discipline, and cold formalities. A worse form of obsession cannot be conceived. The subterfuge, being a superstition, engenders fear, and fear brings the torment of magnetic furies. When we shall have broken the damning charm of superstition, positive in science and character, lifted up in moral sense of rectitude, all devils will depart swiftly as " Legion " into the herd of swine.

HAUNTED HOUSES.

The evidences are too numerous these days to doubt the reality of haunted houses. They have occurred in various places all over the country, unmistakably paralleled by ancient experience. The hallowed quiet of some houses proves the presence of happy angels.

Longfellow has breathed the spiritual conception in the following:

" All houses wherein men have lived and died
　Are haunted houses. Thro' the open doors
　The harmless phantoms on their errands glide,
　　With feet that make no sound upon the floors.

" We meet them at the doorway, on the stair ;
　Along the passages they come and go,
　Impalpable impressions on the air,
　　A sense of something moving to and fro."

In haunted houses voices are often heard, and other noises. In instances of this kind it has been found, generally, the spirits so controlling are not happy. They may be magnetically chained there by some act

of injustice or murder there committed, making the
very walls and furniture of the house a polarized
magnet to operate by.

Among the many items of value in Mrs. Hardinge's
"Spiritualism in America," is the following testimony
from a spirit who averred that he was compelled to
haunt a certain house: "The strongest part of my
earthly magnetism had been poured out in that place;
that crime was strong passion; strong passion ever
liberated strong magnetism; and that human magnetism formed 'tractors,' or magnetic points, which drew
the spiritual body to themselves, and bound it as
forcibly as chains forged in the magnetism of the
universe."

The true way to educe order is to organize a candid
circle with a reliable medium; hold a conversation
with the spirit or spirits, ascertain what is needed,
give wise counsel, and by repeated efforts persuade
into a more harmonious life. This has been repeatedly
done with perfect success.

The most positive magnetic force in a circle rules.
How easy to furnish a preponderance of psychological
thought from the earth plane, and infuse it into the
brain of an honest medium as a genuine communication! This deception has occurred a thousand times,
leading the unwary into difficulty, if the illusion be
followed. This accounts largely for the unreliability
of many communications, and shows the moral necessity of a better adjustment of the magnetic forces on
the part of the inquiring parties, that the spirits may
be the positive battery.

One can see also that it is a very easy matter for a mischievous spirit in the interest of inquiring parties, when they are positive in magnetic control, to work for their interest with wonderful facility. To get at the real merits of such cases, and learn the wishes of the departed, disinterested parties should be employed to form and conduct the circle, and receive the communication.

During our (Senior Editor's) lecture travels, by invitation we attended a spiritual circle in a filthy and disorderly house. The moment the medium was controlled we detected the plane of his obsession. After positive argument and persuasion he consented to leave, averring there was no place for him in the world but that, being shunned by every spirit. We convinced him that his control would ruin the medium and do him (the spirit) also an injury; and that his social odor arose from his soul affections, which, when changed by enlightenment and reform, would win him friends and happiness. He, in departing, thanked us with a resolution to improve. The medium was then influenced by another wiser spirit, who averred that the one we had cast out had lived on earth a vagabond life, and was attracted there by the magnetism of the house, where he had palmed himself off as a distinguished character!

TRANSFIGURATIONS.

When Jesus was on the Mount of Transfiguration, the magnetic cloud there gathered from that circle of

spirits and mediums, became an avenue of articulation,
if we may so credit the testimony.   Undoubtedly
there is a truth here.   The combined sphere of the
circle and whatever belonged to it in association of
interest, was organically materialized into vocal expressions of the spirit's idea.   The same law as to vision
is illustrated by Mrs. Conant, medium for the *Banner
of Light:*

"Certain mediumistic persons who emit from their
bodies a superabundance of magnetic and electric aura
may be called telescopes through which the disem-
bodied spirit can look and behold material objects —
those objects which are as clearly shut out from its
vision as are the objects by which it is surrounded shut
out from yourselves."

Materialization of a spiritual body comes under the
same head.   Allan Kardec, speaking of this law, thus
lucidly sets forth certain statements, which we venture
to be demonstrable in occult science:

"A spirit can, in certain cases, cause it [*périsprit*
or spiritual body] to undergo a species of molecular
modification which renders it visible and tangible to
us; it is thus that apparitions are produced, a phenom-
enon not, in reality, more extraordinary than that of
steam, which is invisible when highly rarified, and
becomes visible when condensed.   *   *   *   It is by
means of its *périsprit* that a spirit acts on and through
its body while living in the material world; it is by
means of this same fluidic intermediary that it mani-
fests itself after the death of the body, by acting on

the inert substances of the material world, producing noises, and the movements of tables, and other objects which it raises, upsets, or carries away. These phenomena should not be deemed surprising, seeing that, even in our sphere, the most powerful motors are precisely those most rarified fluids to which we give the name of 'imponderables,' as air, steam, and electricity. It is also with the aid of its *périsprit* that a spirit causes the medium to write, to draw, to speak, etc. Having no longer a tangible body of its own through which to manifest itself ostensibly, it makes use of the organs of the medium, which it uses as though they were its own, with the aid of the currents of fluidic effluvia which it brings to bear upon him. It is through the actions of these fluidic currents that a spirit moves a table, or causes it to indicate the letters composing the message it wishes to convey. When it raises a table, causing it to float, without visible support, in the air, the spirit does not lift it with arms, but surrounds and penetrates it with a sort of fluidic atmosphere that neutralizes the action of gravitation, exactly as is done by the air in the case of balloons and kites; the fluid with which it is thus saturated gives it, momentarily, a greater specific levity. When a spirit causes a table to adhere to the floor, as though nailed to it, the effect is produced by a process analogous to that by which we produce a vacuum with the aid of the air-pump. When a table moves about the room, the spirit does not move, but merely impels it on its course by directing upon it the action of the jets of fluid that keep it going. When a spirit causes raps in a table, in walls, in other bodies, or in the air, it does not cause them by a blow, but merely directs upon the spot where the rap is heard a jet of fluid that produces the effect of an electric shock. It modifies the sound thus produced, as we modify the sounds produced by the air."

Anna Blackwell thus speaks of spirit pictures: "Those among the people of the fluidic world who are pretty well advanced in the study of substances and forces, are able to produce from those substances, through their skill in directing the action of the formative and qualitative forces, a far greater variety of objects, and of a far higher character, than we can produce in the material sphere; and can also impart to them a variety of qualities — among others that of vitality — which renders their labors interesting and amusing to a degree of which we can form but a very faint idea.

"'I must leave you now,' said a spirit, one day, to a friend of the writer, 'I am busy making a picture, and I want to get on with it.'

"'A picture!' exclaimed my friend, 'I had no idea that spirits could paint pictures, or would care to do anything of the kind!'

"'I said 'a picture,' because I can find no better way of conveying to you something like an idea of what I am making; but it is not at all like what you call a picture in your world, nor do I paint as you paint pictures upon the earth. I work with fluids; and what I make is real and living. I vitalize my flowers, and my animals, and the thousand things I make, so that they are all alive, though not living as such things live in your world; for there is no spirit in them, and they have, therefore, no consciousness, and will only last a short time. Not long ago, in order to receive some friends who were coming to visit me, I made a beautiful arbor, covered with flowers, and full of magnificent singing birds, and it was all living, but only for the short time for which I wanted it. When my friends were gone, I let it melt away again. Those who are more advanced than I am can produce almost any forms or scenery they please, and can make them last longer; but all these things melt away after a time. We never care to keep them long; we should get tired of them. We let them dissolve, and make others.' You cannot imagine how charming these creations are, and how much pleasure we take in them when we are not busy with more serious things.' Spirits say that these fluidic creations are not mere amusements, but that by means of these exercises they gradually learn the properties of substances and of forces, and thus become competent to take part in the direction of the true spirit creations of the material spheres which constitute so important a branch of the occupations of the higher orders of disincarnate intelligences."

EFFECTS OF BIGOTRY.

Obsessed persons of different Christian faiths are often kept in a state of prejudice against Spiritualism and its heavenly ministries by designing and selfish spirits on purpose to prevent their emancipation from their control. We are acquainted with a Universalist of this stamp, who, being morally negative and animal in all his ideas and habits, is perfectly obsessed in every part of his being by low-minded spirits, lest the light will hurt them. Sir Thomas Brown, in his "Religio Medici," conveys similar ideas:

"Those that, to confute their incredulity, desire to see apparitions, shall questionless never behold any. The devil hath them already in a heresy as capital, as witchcraft, and to appear to them were but to convert them."

Obsessional influences are sometimes removed by change of locality. The subjects then come under new magnetisms, which, if not overcome by the controlling spirits, may entirely neutralize the first obsession. Certain localities and houses are more susceptible of spirit influx than others, as with some mineralized mountains and caves, or dwellings long accustomed to the same quality of mediumship.

John Morrison adverts to the fact that when the Scottish mediums change from one country to another, thus coming into new magnetic associations, "their gift is often lost to them."

AN ORTHODOX SPIRIT.

Having heard of the case, we solicited the following. It shows, as in thousands of like conditions, the necessity for a stern and positive action of will—

something that will even shock the unnatural propri-
eties of the obsessed, in order to accomplish a return
to common sense:

"MILWAUKEE, November 18, 1873.

"BROTHER BARRETT: I will now try and redeem the
promise I made you long ago, to give a brief history
of one of the many cases of spirit obsession that have
come under my professional care.

"Mrs. P—— was a lady of very quiet, unpretending
nature, not physically well, but able to attend to the
ordinary household cares. She was brought up under
orthodox influences; was a church-goer, but not mem-
ber; and the neighborhood in which she lived was
thoroughly orthodox. At one of their evening parties
they tried to see what amusement they could get out
of planchette, and, after experimenting, they found it
wrote readily under her hands in response to questions
asked. Soon it astonished them by writing communications and signing names of parties who were long
since dead. Finally it wrote, 'Take the pencil in your
hand,' which she did. Her hand was controlled to
write different communications. Some of the friends
were interested; but many of them, among whom was
her husband, were bitterly opposed to her writing,
while she was much interested. Thus a very inharmonious atmosphere was the result, and she stopped
sitting.

"One day shortly after, she was entranced and lay
for some time in an unconscious condition, in spite
of all their efforts to restore her. All at once she

raised her hands, clasped them, exclaiming, 'I am saved! I am saved! mother has been here, and tells me Spiritualism is all false; have nothing to do with it; cling to the Bible and Jesus!' After which she was so possessed by the belief that she was in direct communion with God, that every impression she received she thought was from Him, and was sure she should shortly die. She ate but little, would allow no fire in the room, although the coldest winter weather, and the windows must be open. In this condition, days followed days, and weeks succeeded weeks; still she was no better, but growing thin in flesh; had her Bible in her hands constantly, and was not at ease unless some one was engaged in prayer. Different physicians were consulted, but they could not agree as to her disease, some calling it softening of the brain, others insanity; and arrangements were in progress to take her to the Insane Asylum.

"The minister of the church she attended visited her, prayed with her, and finally pronounced her converted! Time wore on, and the family being worried out with sleepless nights and witnessing her distressed condition, sent for me. When I saw her she looked more like a corpse than a living woman. As I came to her bedside she looked up, saying, 'It is no use, doctor; God and Jesus tell me I have got to die.' I replied, 'I am more than a match for your God and the devil both; you can't die if I am here.' And I joked her, laughed, and kept up such a constant sally that she soon became mirthful. In the mean time I kept my will active to get possession of her, and dispossess the controlling spirit. Gradually I succeeded, until I had her just as thoroughly under my psychological control as she had been under the other's, and I assure you at this time she thought far less of the Bible and praying ' for Christ's sake.' After having her thus under my influence, I told her why she had felt as she had; told her she was possessed by an ignorant, orthodox spirit, who was killing her, not by intent, but through selfishness; and that she must try and resist the influence. She kept in this quiet, rational frame of mind for some time after I left, but finally the orthodox control again took her, and before it could be permanently overcome she had to be removed from the house and entire surroundings. After getting away entirely from the magnetic sphere she had been in, she was restored, and different spirits came and influenced her, and she is now a good test medium.

" If this should meet her eye, she will please excuse me for thus putting her case before the public for the sake of the lessons that may be culled therefrom, which are:

" *First* — That irregular and disorderly control generally comes to those who are not posted in spiritual laws, and opposing elements being brought to bear upon the sensitive.

"*Second* — That there are those, in spirit life as well as here, who do not believe in spirit communion, and are opposed thereto; and that knowledge of spirit life and the laws relating to spiritual existence are the

14

only means of safety, and that harmonious surround
ings are necessary to all sensitives during the stage of
developing into an acting medium. Ignorance is the
source of all the trouble in this direction, causing
untold suffering, often resulting in permanent insanity;
and that knowledge of, and a regard for, all the laws
of our being, both spiritual and physical, is our only
savior.   JULIET H. SEVERANCE, M. D."

INTEMPERATE SPIRITS.

Judge Edmonds — perhaps no man in the ranks of
Spiritualists has had experiences so diverse and deep
as this gentleman, now an ascended seer and ministering angel. He embraced Spiritualism on its
birth-morn in this country, and for more than a score
of years has been a critical investigator and able
defender of it in its phenomenal and philosophical
aspects. Studying law in the office of President Van-
Buren, practicing in the courts, counseling in important cases, revising the statute laws of New York,
occupying a high judicial position seventeen years,
accustoming himself to the sifting of evidence all this
time, prepared him for the study of Spiritualism in
all its psychological ramifications. Serving as Circuit
Judge for several years, he was further honored with
a seat upon the Bench of the Supreme Court. While
occupying this distinguished position he was spirit-
itually gifted with clairvoyance and clairaudience.
The great "clemency" which he was sometimes
charged with showing to criminals was owing to his
clairvoyant and spiritual perceptions of the causes

that led to misfortunes and crimes. Evidently many criminals are led into their dark deeds by spirits peopling the lower spheres. This, though modifying, does not abrogate moral responsibility.

The Judge has recently expressed the opinion that many of the so-called lunatics in asylums are only under the influence of spirits. "Some fifteen cases of insanity, or rather obsession," says the Judge, " I have been instrumental in curing. This I said to the Academy of Science, in New York."

During a recent visit to New York the Judge, then in earth form, related to us this incident, in substance as here described. Well does it illustrate the law already defined, that mental conditions alike attract, sometimes producing unintentional and unconscious obsession:

" A professional gentleman of the city, engaged in the law, and an exemplary Christian, walking, as he believed, in the fear of God, of a sudden became irritable, cross in his family, inclined to swear, and what was more strange to himself, he at times thirsted for liquor. He became daily more and more a puzzle to himself. Though a temperance man all his life, he could hardly get by a dram-shop without going in, and though ever cautious in language, he could hardly keep at times from swearing outrageously; and then he was tempted in other directions not necessary to name. At times he felt suspicious, selfish, and utterly unlike himself every way. His family observed how strange he acted, and then he became magnetically nervous and angered at the least provocation, so unlike his previous calm, upright and moral life."

Finally he felt inclined to consult Judge Edmonds. Calling upon him, and commencing to relate his condition in a round-about way, the Judge said: "You tell me no more; I know all about it. A spirit came into the room with you — a spirit who is the cause, unknown to you, of all your troubles."

"What spirit?" inquired this attorney.

"He does not give me his name," replied the Judge, "but has been relating his history. It seems from his appearance and what he says, that he was an ignorant and positive, a selfish and worldly man, who went to California in the gold fever days. He lived on the lower plane of California mining life. In the mines he died. He tells me that he remained about the mines sometime — remained or lingered in the *dark*. He was neither happy nor very miserable. He seemed to be pretty much alone, and yet he was conscious of other and better beings about him, who did not come to him. Dissatisfied with his locality and condition, he resolved to go back East — to New York — and about the first one he saw, or saw clearly enough to come into sympathetic relations with, was you."

"What did he come to me for," asked this Christian attorney, shuddering at the thought. "What sympathy could there be?"

"He says," replied the Judge, "you were suffering with the same physical disease that he died with, and your dissatisfaction and mental irritability, caused by the physical disease attracted him to you."

"But what do you stay with me for," asked the lawyer.

"Because I like to," was the spirit's reply.

"Why do you like to?"

"Because it is light around you; and then I can better hear and know what is going on in the world, that I did not want to leave."

This obsessed lawyer and the obsessing spirit (through Judge Edmonds) then held a long conversation.

Finally the Judge, who was both clairvoyant and clairaudient at the time, talked to the spirit kindly and friendly, telling him what to do — to leave the man, to look up, to pray, to ask the aid of God and angels for light, etc.

"In a few weeks," said the Judge, "I met this lawyer again, and said: Well, how do you get along?"

"Oh, finely; my health is good, and I have felt no desire to be profane, or to turn into the gin-shops along the streets."

"Of course, you feel finely," replied the Judge; "for that spirit has been hanging about me more or less, half obsessing *me*. Actually, for several days the electric aura that he threw around me in his efforts to stay with me made me cross when I had no occasion for it, inclined me, for the moment, to profanity, and cold-hearted selfishness, and other vices. Seeing that I would not yield, and at the same time willing him to depart, together with reliance upon my angel helpers, he left." The Judge added that "a denial of obsessions is a confession of ignorance touching the

psychological effects of mind upon mind, and spheres
infringing upon spheres."

The Judge has had Catholic priests, after a thorough
trial of their "holy water and prayers," send their
mediumistic members, when wickedly disordered, to
be demagnetized and released from the grasp of
obsessional spirits.

During our recent visit to India an English officer
told us certain facts respecting the method of casting
out evil spirits by the Brahmins of the present day:

North and east of Benares, the Sacred City of the
Hindoos, is a mountain consecrated to the relief of the
obsessed. The little city of Andipore, at the foot of
this mountain, is often thronged by the obsessed,
sent thither by the Brahmins to be dispossessed of
their demons. Through this city runs the river
Kistna. Up the sides of the mountain are boarding
houses, and cells for the more unfortunate. Tradition
says this mountain is holy, from having been "breathed
upon by the gods." All admit the location to be
retired and healthy. The obsessed are required to be
abstemious in diet, bathe three times a day, repeating
Brahminical prayers while bathing. Then they form
a circle around the victim of the demon, the holiest of
the priests vigorously pathetising him, and the
remainder chanting prayers for the gods to take possession. Finally the priest puts forehead to forehead,
knee to knee, mouth to mouth, and breathes or "blows"
away the demon, saying holy words.

INJURY OF SUDDEN EXPULSION.

When an obsessing spirit has full and perfect control of its subject, a sudden dispossession may be injurious to the life of the subject. The New Testament states several instances where Jesus cast out the evil spirits, that they tore their subjects, and on leaving them " left them as dead." A battle of course ensues, where two powerful batteries of will are thus exerted upon each other, and the peril falls most upon the person possessed. Cases are on record, occurring frequently, where the charmed bird falls at the shot that kills the obsessing snake. How much more potent is the psychological force that holds the delicate organism of a medium.

As the true object should be in all dispossessions to benefit both the spirit and its subject, the wiser course to pursue is to enter into conversation with the spirit, instructively and kindly and firmly citing to a better life and the natural ways for attaining it, and so persuade the spirit away. Speak to the obsessing powers as men, brothers, friends — reason with them as members of a common Father's family, and, at the same time demagnetizing the subject, bring a healthier, purer magnetism, and calmer, higher and more elevating influences to the patient's relief.

Obsessions being adverse, inauspicious, psychological influences cast upon the organism — being the thoughts and feelings of individuals controlled by such spirits as are necessitated in accordance with the immutable laws of compensation to range for a season the lower planes of life — the preventive lies in good health, good nature, and a good life; in the cultivation of broad, loving, aspirational aims, a firmness of moral principles, a determined purpose to do, dare, live the right, a calm trust in the overshadowing presence of the Infinite, and the holy watch-care of those beautiful angels that delight to do the will of heaven. Ill health, nervous affections, dejection, despair, suspicion, jealousies, expose the subject to obsessions, or they offer suitable conditions for demons inclined to fun, mischief or base schemings, to carry out their selfish plans. Truth attracts the true, wisdom the wise, love the lovely, charity the charitable, and purity the pure of all worlds.

The virtue of a strong moral will of kindness was beautifully illustrated in an experience of the editor of the *Banner of Light*, Luther Colby. An Indian spirit visited him in the most ferocious manner, determined to do mischief. Mr. Colby was calm, reasoned with him, persuaded him, and finally won his confidence, and afterward he became a most useful visitant in his band, rendering him essential service in many instances of peril and need.

CURING BY MUSIC.

" Music hath charms," it is said, " to calm the savage breast." Who has not felt its power over despondency and even disease? Its love-notes are an all-cure to the soul. And if that music be of the spirits come to soothe us, who can resist its divinity? There is a legend that in an ancient city, when the bell of the temple rung, the " offending genii " took flight. There is a morality in music most potent in reforms, as the effect of popular songs upon society plainly indicates. Jamblichus, understanding this moral ratio, says in substance, that the melodies of the gods "insinuate themselves inspirationally into our spirits, and wholly work in us by their musical essences and power." We have a case in point recorded in the Old Testament (1 Samuel), wherein it is stated that the harp-playing of David dispossessed King Saul of an evil spirit:

"And it came to pass, when the *evil* spirit from God was upon Saul, that David took an harp, and played with his hand: so Saul was refreshed, and was well, and the evil spirit departed from him."

"Return no more, vain bodings of the night!
  A happier oracle within my soul
Hath swelled to power; a clear unvarying light
  Mounts thro' the battling clouds that round me roll,
    And to a new control
  Nature's full harp gives forth rejoicing tones,
  Wherein my glad sense owns
The accordant rush of elemental sound
To one consummate harmony profound;
  One grand creation hymn,
  Whose notes the seraphim
Lift to the glorious height of music winged and crowned."

15

CHAPTER IX.

SPIRITS can do nothing outside of nature. Indeed there is no place to stand outside. Whatever mortals do, spirits aid. Need we puzzle our brains with the effort to distinguish which is mortal and which is spiritual agency? As well might we try to decide what part in the growth of a plant is attributable to the sun, what to the soil, what to the air, what to electricity. We have no chemistry to analyze here. All nature is a unit; all forces blend as do drops in the ocean. Does not a touch upon any part of the human body affect the whole? Does not a little thought communicate itself to every nerve in the system?

A spirit is virtually present wherever any of its acts or relics exist, or its sympathy extends. Take a bar of magnetized steel; divide or subdivide; each piece is a distinct magnet. Separate them ten feet, a hundred, a thousand, a mile, any distance; do we thus destroy the reciprocal relation? Mind is inseparable from its history. Between the mind and its sequences is an eternal union. What is memory but the registry of thought? Its record leaves are endless. Persons resuscitated from the drowning state aver that the

(170)

experiences of life flash before them in a moment.
What a solemn truth here! How pathetically plead
the very hours we live, to dot upon the soul beautiful
deeds! Nothing, then, is plainer than that we *never*
can be separated from each other. All is one vast
immortality. What if we pass away into the realm
of spirit; the memory lives and brightens with use;
and the sympathy is stronger than before, for the soul
yearns after its counterpart to meet externally as they
constantly meet internally. The separated spirit
lingers in love with all the objects it has lived with.
Yesterday the sun bathed all the landscape in light,
and every particle of ground and drop of water was
fused with its golden magnetism. Was the sympathy
destroyed when the sun went down? Everything
turned a face sunward, seeking it, and in the effort to
get close to it, crowding its fellow forward, there is a
circuit of the earth round and round. Friends departed
and friends remaining are intuitively drawn to each
other. A lock of hair left, a picture, a letter, or name,
anything ever associated with and polarized by the
departed, has the imprint of the very love and thought
of that revered friend. Spirit writing is never effaced.
These things ever seek their magnetizer — the spirit
gone; and to them that spirit is unconsciously, or con-
sciously, sending forth a responsive influence. They
never cease to be talismans of loving communication,
because they are magnetically fed the same as the
earth by the ever-burning sun. Hence, when we
psychometrically touch such a relic, we are instantly
put in rapport with the spirit that once magnetized it.

MULTIFORM CONTROL.

It is well known to every magnetizer, well skilled in his profession, that he can bring a large percentage of any congregation under his control, and make such think, feel and act alike; that when his subjects are in perfect rapport with him, he can control them without respect to distances; and that thus sick patients can be healed. The same law holds good with ministering spirits. Benjamin Franklin, or Black Hawk, for instance, can have his scores of mediums in the earth life, and at will can influence one or all of them at once, though in different parts of the world. If the sympathy is perfect, they are influenced without the volition of the spirit; that is, being enveloped in his spiritual sphere, they imbibe his thought, and understand his purposes, for they and he are one in the circle of life. Thus a dozen, or any number, of communications can be given at the same time to different media. The ruling spirit may also send as many representatives as he has circles, and essentially it would be the same as if present himself personally, for the will and thought of spirits on the same plane and in the same band, are in harmony.

"Why can I not communicate with my own dear friend departed without the foreign agency of a medium?" This question is often asked. In the earth sphere friendships are formed principally on the external, material plane. Association, self-interest, organic sympathy, and other outward relations may induce endearments which at first experience may appear to be lasting; but absence, distance, and changes of magnetisms sometimes cancel these affections. Nothing is enduring which is not spiritual. If, then, a friend, having passed the ordeal of death, has organized his basis of love on the spiritual plane, and the earth-friend remains, as before, wholly external, the difference of condition amounts to a magnetic gulf that cannot be passed over except by mediation. A medium contains, in organization, the blended elements of physical and spiritual natures, and is able, therefore, to conjoin the two parties for exchange of language by word or sign. The medium is the bridge or telegraph that spans from the internal spiritual to the external sensuous. When, then, so wide a conditional difference exists, is not a medium necessary before any tangible communication can be opened up between the two worlds?

The spiritual batteries are very delicate; the least agitation of mind disturbs them and dilutes or perverts the truthfulness of the oracles; hence the absolute need of candor, calmness and a childlike sincerity of purpose. If a weeping mother is over-anxious, she may thus defeat her object. If she is mediumistic, in such a state she can do nothing; a medium of less intensity of feeling is needed to restore order and open intercourse.

It is a well known fact, demonstrable in all spiritual circles, or in the action of artificial batteries, that they are operative to success· only when the forces are in order — positive with negative and negative with positive. Great anxiety, fear, doubt, may produce a general confusion when all phenomena are destroyed; so if the inquirer is very willful, stubborn and positively repulsive. Excessive grief, despair or hopeless mourning, naturally engendering discordant states, will neutralize the phenomena by absorption.

NATURAL AND ACQUIRED MEDIUMSHIP.

Mediumship is constitutional, does not depend on moral character, is often a birth right quality, and is acquirable by culture through the aid of circles. Where the mediumistic powers — which all more or less possess — are latent or undeveloped, it may require long months and years of persistent effort to become receptive direct of spiritual influx. We know of persons who have sat for a full year without a sign, at first, of spirit presence; but by perseverance at last removed the natural obstructions, or spiritualized the nervous system to the direct perception of spirits. The first victory to gain is putting oneself in a state of spiritual balance, and it comes when we faithfully attend to the conditions.

Respecting the capability of a person's entering into intercourse with spirits, Jung Stilling says:

"*First* — A natural disposition to it consists in this: When the ethereal part or luminous body of the human soul does not imbibe many heavy particles from the blood, but keeps itself pure; by which means it borders more closely upon the invisible world. This, however, does not depend on the will of man, but on the internal organization of the body.

" *Second* — When the luminous body of the human soul receives any particular accumulation of power, so that it becomes more active than is necessary for life and sensation; it may then happen that the individual may appear in the invisible world and have intercourse with its inhabitants."

ABUSES OF MEDIUMSHIP.

Nothing is more perilous to health and morals than bigoted prejudices and oppositions against mediumship in a family or among friends. The medium is then in a cross-fire between forces, producing a smothered condition of mind that in time reacts upon the whole body. Often do we find media entirely broken down and hopeless, and morally helpless, when long subjected to such discords. In the general confusion, should the opposing influences prevail, the medium becomes diseasedly negative, when some spirit of the same grade of character, to fill the painful vacuum, may take possession and hold a sullen and melancholic control here locked as in " chains of darkness."

How many of us have learned the law, and yet how few practice it, that a positive skeptical mind, thinking to detect fraud, silently neutralizes the magnetic current and deprives the medium of all power to act for the time being. Another fact must be considered, that media, being negative, live two lives, internal and external, and liable to be ensnared by almost any influence of a positive nature, sometimes seemingly unfaithful to one's sense and to a betrayal thereof, while

the true cause may lie in an influence unseen. Trace
to the cause and we shall find just grounds for a world
of charity.

ORDERLY CIRCLES.

All the powers of our being should be mediumized,
if we would indeed be spiritual. We need our sacred
hours when we can enter the closet of the soul for
communion with the heavenly intelligences. Such a
circle with one or two others, or even alone, is often
the best. A promiscuous or dissonant circle is perilous
to health and good morals. It jars and scatters. An
orderly circle, having similarity of spheres as to
planes, but variegated in electrical action to awaken
inspiring influences, is characterized by sincere purposes, with strict attention to temperamental and
psychological laws.

The plane of the aggregated affections of the inquirers molds the quality of the communication. We
get what we seek. Every organ of the brain, and of
the whole being in fact, ever emiting its corresponding magnetic sphere, calls for and receives its proper
response. The orderly adjustment of these multiform
forces is, therefore, very delicate.

If possible, assemble in the same consecrated room
once or twice a week, not oftener, around the same
table, with the same company at first, until the battery
is strong enough to endure the presence of strangers
without neutralizing the control. Such circles should
also be regular. Have a journal kept of each meeting.

Reading sometimes in a spiritual train of thought, singing, and vocal or silent invocation, are essential helps. Avoid intellectual disputations, for they engender positive conditions, defeating the object. The moment a circle becomes monotonous, repellant or dozy, stop all operations, disband for a short time, till the electric forces are quickened again, when the experiment may be repeated, this time perhaps with success. Above all things, avoid too long sessions One hour of close attention, with lively feelings and affections, may be a safe rule.

Phenomena should not be the main object, but simply the incidents. Even if no rappings or other manifestations occur, it is a beautiful success, provided the aspiration is holy. Spirits will reveal themselves in multiform proofs of their presence whenever we comply with the laws of an exalted mediumship.

DISORDERLY CIRCLES.

A disorderly spiritual circle, established from curiosity, attractive to itself by passional demands, with no higher aim than to "get the manifestations," with no moral ambition to be better in life for the spiritual intercourse, is in fact the most subtile peril that can possibly entangle the unwary. We are not surprised that Dr. Edward Beecher, unfortunately observing only the perverse kind, and thence from prejudices refusing to investigate the good of orderly circles, so emphatically criticised what he saw and felt:

"Colorless daylight does not enter that fane; a

sepulchral taint sickens the atmosphere, and he who has not by effort and practice gained command over himself, exclaims, 'If I stay long in this place I shall lose my senses; let me escape from it while I can.' "

Had Mr. Beecher been as wise here as he is even in his church relations, "proving all things," condemning no cause because it is so abused, he would have had large credit for this angelic method of communication.

DARK CIRCLES.

Why does the photographer develop his pictures in the dark? The fact is, light is the neutralizer of his chemical designs. Some maintain that the human eye, being a powerful magnetizer, acts precisely upon the processes of *spiritual* chemistry or phenomena, as light does upon the incipient photograph.

Night is the negative state of nature, receptive of influences necessary to recuperation. Man's positive labors closed, his mind, enveloped in the solemn silence all around him, driving the forces of the senses to their centres, engendering reflections upon death and the "world to come," is better conditioned to receive spiritual impression. If he is calm, trustful, truth-loving — the initial of heavenly communings — trooping angels, obedient to his inmost prayer, respond in revelations. During the day they are not so much needed, for then all our powers are active, on the alert, watching, planning, executing; but at night the intellectual brain sinks down in its beautiful temple for repose, and the spiritual affections, more free, rise to greet the guardian visitants, to bask in the celestial sunshine, to wander in dreams and visions, and poise themselves on some holy mountain of thought, prophet-like, preparatory for practical work.

Says Dr. N. B. Wolfe, author of "Startling Facts in Modern Spiritualism:" "In the absence of solar rays the integuments of the eye become so highly sensitized that they develop a more perfect luminous condition than they can in the face of day. Thus the dark room becomes to the eye what the dark tube of the microscope becomes to sight — an augmentive power, which reveals the wonderful phenomena of millions of creatures in a dewdrop. The telescope, in like manner, with its lenses and dark chamber, assists the eye to penetrate space so remote that the added power makes the senses ache. Telescope the earth, and from the bottom of a well you may see stars at the high noon of day."

It may be of some utility to the inquirer here to state that most of the spiritual phenomena of the Bible was produced in the night, thus showing a perfect parallel between the ancient and modern, centralizing in immutable law, repeatable in effect under similar conditions and necessities.

At night Jesus had his heavenly worship; at night he calmed the stormy sea of Tiberias; at night he walked upon its waves; at night the prison doors opened by the power of spirits to emancipate Peter; at night the stone was rolled from the sepulchre, and the crucified came forth, conquerer of "death and hell."

Dark circles do not incidentally imply dark spirits.

The good can be trusted at all times. If tricksters abuse our confidence, it is no reason that we should ignore a natural law, or cease to use it in conversion. Let us not judge principles by human actions. If we have been deceived, why, all is, be more vigilant in the right. The underlying science is not harmed by any humbugs. If even one suffering mortal, long wandering in the gloom of atheism, can, in a dark circle, catch the faintest view of the star of immortal hope, it is worth a world to him. We ought not to be indifferent to others' claims for occular evidence.

We sincerely believe, however, that the dark must give place, largely, to the light circle. No truth need long be hidden. The fact that some phases of the spiritual phenomena can be produced in the light is a sure augury of honest sunshine by and by.

A PLEA FOR THE MEDIUMS.

Suppose we were to abolish the postoffice system, or the telegraph, and depend upon the chances of travel for communication, would it not be a retrogression against which every person in the land would revolt? Suppose the opposers of spiritual ministry should succeed in putting down all the mediums in the country, and in driving the spirits back, leaving the world only what it had before, only the traditions and symbols of immortality, what would be the loss? The very thought of thus blotting out forever all the heavenly phenomena from mankind is most painful.

Mediumship is the spiritual postoffice, the telegraph, the oceanic cable of love that marries this life with the life to come. By it immortality has been demonstrated, the sorrowing consoled, the benighted enlightened, the dying rejoiced, the bereft blessed with unspeakable gladness, the diseased healed, the reformers of a new age projected. It pertains to all grades of human life, connects with all hearts, and is as general to our suffering humanity as are nerves in the physical system. No price can parallel its value; no language can paint its moral virtue, when rightly applied; no angel can tell what blessedness it brings to the children of earth. We allow there are deceptions unavoidably associated as parasites with mediumship, but we aver there are less in fact than in other departments of our religious life. Compare it with the solemn mockery and cant of formal worship, or the hypocrisy that lurks under the garb of ecclesiastic respectability.

The success of mediumship depends very much upon faith, or confidence in the parties operating. Delicate to the touch of a thought, subject to all the magnetisms around it, liable by the least will-force to be diverted from a straight course of news-telling from the heavenly shore, it is indeed a wonder there is no more ambiguity or uncertainty in the communications. It shows the moral potency of angelic control, and the secure hope it brings of ultimate triumph for reliable revelations. If believers cultivate doubt, and blast their own instruments of industry, what result can we expect but that the jeering world, aiding the destruction of heavenly commerce, will gloat as devils over fallen angels plunged to the hell of atheism again?

Many a poor medium has been pressed unconsciously
and unintentionally to assist the spirits when conditions produced by repulsions were unfavorable.
Reputed as having a most contemptible profession,
many a chosen one in a moment of despair has cut the
silver telegraphing that connects with the divine, and
sunk back bleeding and fainting in spiritual darkness.
Who shall write accurately what inward pains the
mediums have endured; what persecutions have slain
best affections; what injustice has stabbed their hearts?
There are experiences here revealing the truth that
"fact is stranger than fiction." "In secret have I
said nothing," is the answer of the maligned to the
crucifiers. If anything is to be pardoned in our world,
it is that mediumship which is by force of magnetic
piracy *compelled* to be a blind leader of the blind. A
kind word, a loving confidence, a defensive attitude
around our mediums, will entwine them with wreaths
of moral beauty. We plead for the mediums. Tell it
round the world, publish it in the Summer-Land, that
the mediums must be, and shall be, defended and pro-
tected, loved and appreciated, succored and rewarded,
as laborers worthy of their hire.

UNMEDIATED SPIRITUALITY.

Infancy is a dependency — cared for by another — a
physical mediumship. In subsequent years the once-
child, now a man, assumes an independent action, is a
supplier in turn, a ministrant. It should be so with
our spiritual growth. Our first step here is the phenomenal, essential to knowledge as the nine digits to

hematics. But it would be just as consistent to confine a scholar to a commutation of these figures for amusement, as to be continuously chasing mere appearances. If this were all, what the profit? What the *moral* gain from rope-tying, rapping, the psychic play of automatic brain, or anything else of the kind? They are only signs — husks of the ripening corn. The soul must be fed on adaptable food; but if here starved, being *alone* but little better than theology, it must in time madden its best affections. The phenomenal is physical, appeals to the sensuous, invites the grosser, enriches here as a garden *prepared* for the planting; but if wanting in moral protection and culture, it surely is infested with weeds, nerve fevers, passional promiscuities, and obsessional relations that give the face a demoniac look, glazed eyes, and famished expressions — the mad stare of spiritual insanity. Let facts all around us decide the matter! We have yet to find a solitary, *happy* Spiritualist who can furnish no stronger evidence of his enlightenment than contortions of muscles or the concussions of electric forces by the raps that come simply to arrest attention; and it is a questionable morality in Spiritualism if the best communications one receives are profane and vulgar. True, all this evidences a life beyond, that it but continues this life, retaining the legitimate effects of rudimental inversions, and so far should warn us how we use our precious gifts; but when, as very many professed Spiritualists do, such communications are sought and invited with a chuckling ribaldry, without

the least effort or inclination on the part of the inquirers to demand the reformation of such spirits, themselves
the patterns first, it is a wonder that their souls do not
rot with their impure bodies ere death gravitates them
more directly to the plane they have established.
Write it down, write it indelibly upon the memories
of the coming generation of Spiritualists, that phenomenal Spiritualism, with its sensuous associations,
is as essential to progress as steam to an engine; but
write it so legibly as *never* to be forgotten, that without moral courage and conscientious intelligence
cultivated and practiced, this spiritual steam becomes
our greater and swifter ruin!   And write in letters of
flaming light, like that which startled Belshazzar and
his companionable revellers, when a spirit hand traced
the fiery sentence: "Mene, mene, tekel, upharsin —
*Thou art weighed in the balances, and art found
wanting!*" that a sensuous mediumship, careless of
responsibility, brings a mixed multitude of spirits that
will "enter in" and make such an organism a living
tomb, "full of dead men's bones and of all uncleanness."
No lofty character has yet been developed here.   It is
an impossibility.   A sensuous mediumship, rightly
related, is not a finality, but a ministrant, the same as
the body should be to the spirit.   To accomplish the
design of wise spirits in thus opening the heavens
upon earth in *tangible* proof of immortality, the phenomenal *should* be preserved in active culture as a
rudimental process; but when the inquirers are thus
convinced, a further continuance of such evidences

to them becomes a forced invite to spirits, and so an obsession. There is something ahead of this, and if not sought and attained, that soul is the worse imprisoned for such control. As the flash and destruction of electricity from the cloud enters into the growth of vegetation and animal life, so must phenomenal Spiritualism, though repeating itself from age to age, merge into a more exalted configuration of intellectual and moral character, and there be no longer phenomenal, but a silent presence of the holy angel. Any other Spiritualism is an abortion—a spiritual disease and death!

There is, then, an unmediated spirituality, when evidences come direct to us personally, when a second or third individual, so far from aiding us, casts a shadow, and so obscures the brighter vision. Every soul possesses innately a capacity to be in the fullness of time a focus of all immortalities of love and truth; to be a god verily, as Jesus was, who, when unmediated, or thoroughly spiritualized, could honestly say: "All power is given me in heaven and in earth." The beloved apostle, John, spoke of this attainment thus: "I was in the spirit on the Lord's day." Buddha spoke of it as a heart that has "penetrated the deep principles of universal mind." Christna is represented as calling it an "eternal absorption into the divine nature." Our Davis, "the Poughkeepsie seer," happily styles it "The Superior State." It is indeed the unmediated celestial experience, when immortality has a breathing in our very consciousness.

16

CHAPTER X.

THE spiritual philosophy puts into the hand of investigators the key which unlocks the mysteries of the past and the marvels of the present. Wherever Bibles have been written, or prophets have lived; wherever seers have been illumined or saints walked and worshiped; wherever the dreamer has dreamed of a coming Eden, and freedom sung of a millenial era; wherever a great mind or a combination of great minds have lifted the waiting souls of generations into a higher civilization, there was the vitalizing element of Spiritualism.

Man is a worshiping being. He instinctively adores the ancient, the experienced, the wise, the good, the beautiful. This is the dome of his life, the highest and best, for which all other service is disciplinary. Without it man is not man. With his intellectual and passional nature, though never so large, he cannot pass over to the "Most High" if the arch of his spiritual and reverential is not erected from the seen into the unseen, as a bridge from shore to shore.

"The universe," says J. Burns, of England, " is in every part alive, and has been living and thriving ever and ever. Everything in it is alive, and all members

(186)

and portions of it are ceaselessly and industriously hand in hand, with one aim and purpose, developing forms of life, life, life. There is no dead matter: all is animated with a great, intelligent, self-regulating soul; and we cannot imagine a time when this state of things did not exist; when ideas from this interior, intelligent fountain were not being incarnated in forms and perpetuating an independent individual existence, types of the great original. Granting, then, this' eternity of being to be a fact—that the illimitable, intelligent, vital, and divine vortex of all that forms, animates, and energizes has flowed on forever through matter, its external body or receptive principle — then we have an incessant series of vital forms, the result of the conjoined action of Father God, the positive or male principle, and Mother Nature, the receptive or female principle."

No greater mistake can writers of the Christian or anti-Christian schools make than when they aver from historic records that the religious races, Biblical or classic, have ever taught an abstract Polytheism disconnected from the Monotheistic idea. Is it not a very superficial comprehension of the deeps of human mind, or its natural intuition, to conclude it is idolatrous, or Polytheistic, because its conception of God is limited exactly to the measure of its capacity? What is the ideal, even of the most expanded intelligence, but limited to finite relations? What are the clothings of principles, whether ideal or visibly substantial, but finites? Living in a world of forms — forever living there — where impersonal principles are organized, and therefore limited in space, we instinctively institute religious systems correspondingly circumscribed, just as we are mentally and affectionally keyed in degree of unfoldment.

THE TRANSCENDENT LAW.

The idea of God is germinal in the human soul. It is traceable through all the forms of Fetishism, Sabeism, Polytheism, and Monotheism, to pure Theism, culminating in the Spiritualistic idea of to-day, of a divine paternity and maternity, "who is above all, through all, and in us all." What Christians have bigotedly accused the heathen of as idolatrous, was ever to them but symbols of the Infinite, as forming itself in their constructive imaginations. Thus, an English missionary relates that, standing with a venerable Brahmin to witness the sacred images carried in pomp and cast into the Ganges, he said:

"Behold your gods; made with hands; thrown into a river."

"What are they, sir?" replied the Brahmin. "Only dolls! That is well enough for the ignorant, but not for the wise."

And he went on to quote from the ancient Hindoo laws of Menu:

"The world lay in darkness, as asleep. Then He who exists for Himself, the Most High, the Almighty, manifested Himself and dispelled the gloom. He whose nature is beyond our reach, whose being escapes our senses, who is invisible but eternal — He, the all-pervading Spirit, whom the mind cannot grasp, even He shone forth."

Says Rev. Samuel Longfellow: "Wherever Polytheism has prevailed there has been a vague sense of unity accompanying it and growing clearer with growing intelligence. One of the gods comes to be regarded as supreme, and the others to be but his ministers or angels. The Jehovah of the Jews appears at first to have been conceived of as not the only God, but the special God of their nation, superior to the gods of the other nations. Thus, even in Homer, we find a tendency to gather up into Zeus as centre and source all the functions of the other divinities.

"The Egyptians believed in a 'first God; being before all, and alone; fountain of all.'

"The Aztecs, of Mexico, with their more than two hundred deities, recognized one Supreme Creator and Lord, whom they addressed in their prayers as 'the God by whom we live,' 'omnipresent, that knoweth all thoughts, and giveth all gifts,' 'without whom man is as nothing,' 'invisible, incorporeal; one God, of perfect perfection and purity.'

"So the ancient Peruvians had their 'Creator and Sustainer of Life;' the American Indians their Great Spirit, 'Master of Life;' the Scandinavians their All-Father.

"And where the forms of polytheistic mythology occupied the popular mind, the intelligent and philo-

sophic have always regarded these as but the shapes
of fancy, and taught a pure doctrine of the unity and
spirituality of God. Socrates tells of the joy with
which he read in a book of Anaxagoras, that the universe was a creation of Mind. And Xenophanes, as
Aristotle relates, casting his eyes upward to the heavens, declared the One is God. He condemned the
prevalent mythologies and the notions of gods in
human figure, and severely blamed Hesiod and Homer
for their scandalous tales about the gods. He taught
that 'there is one supreme God among beings divine
and human. * * * He governs all things by the
power of reason.'

"The Pythagoreans taught the unity of God, and
compared him to a circle whose centre is everywhere,
whose circumference nowhere.

"'There are not different gods for different nations,'
wrote Plutarch. 'As there is one and the same sun,
moon, sky, earth, and sea for all men, though they call
them by different names, so the One Spirit which governs this universe, the Universal Providence, receives
among different nations different names.'

"'There is but one God, who is everywhere,' says
Marcus Aurelius, the Roman Emperor.

"'God is everywhere,' wrote an Aztec mother to
her daughter.

"'In all this conflict of opinions,' says Maximus
Tyrius, 'know that through all the world sounds one
consenting law and idea, that there is one God, the

King and Father of all, and many gods, the children of God. This both the Greek and the Barbarian teach.'

"The Hindu, 'Bhagavad Gita,' speaks of 'the Supreme, Universal Spirit, the Eternal Person, divine, before all gods, omnipresent. Creator and Lord of all that exists; God of gods, Lord of the universe.' In a Buddhist tract we read: 'There appears in the law of Buddha only one Omnipotent Being.' And again, 'He is a Supreme Being above all others; and although there are many gods, yet there is a Supreme who is God of the gods.' Huc relates a conversation with a Thibetan Lama, who said to him: 'We must not confound religious truth with the superstitions which amuse the credulity of the ignorant. There is but one sole Sovereign Being, who has created all things. He is without beginning, and without end: He is without body, He is a spiritual substance.'

"In the Mazdean, or Zoroastrian belief, Ormuzd is spoken of as 'omniscient, omnipotent, and omnipresent; formless, self-existent, and eternal; pure and holy; Lord over all the creatures in the universe; the refuge of those who seek his aid.'

"Upon a temple at Delphi was the inscription *Et*=Thou art. And upon this Plutarch writes, 'We say to God, Thou art: giving Him thus His true name, the name which belongs alone to Him. For what truly *is?* That which is eternal, which has never had beginning by birth, never will have end by death, that to which time brings no change. It would be wrong to say of *Him who is*, that He was or will be, for these words express changes and vicissitudes. God alone *is:* He is, not after the fashion of things measured by time, but by an immovable and unchanging eternity. For Him there is no *before* nor *after*, but by a single *now* he fills the *forever*. And nothing truly is but He alone!'

"Again, after denying the fable of the birth and education of Jove, Plutarch says: 'There is nothing before Him, He is the first and most ancient of beings, the author of all things: He was from the beginning; too great to owe his existence to any other than himself. From his sight is nothing hid. * * * Night and slumber never weigh upon that infinite eye, which alone looks upon the truth. By Him we see, by Him we have all which we possess. Giver of all good, ordainer of all which is, and which happens, it is He who gives all and makes all. In Him are the beginning, the end, the measure, the destiny of every thing.' "

"The name Father is used as familiarly in the Hindoo hymns as in the Christian. Thus, in the Rig Veda: 'May our Father, Heaven, be favorable to us; may that Eternal One protect us evermore. We have no other friend, no other Father.' * * * 'The Father of Heaven, who is the Father of men.'

"'Father of gods and of men,' says Hesiod, of Zeus. Homer repeats it. A similar recognition of a Supreme Paternity is mentioned by Horace, Plutarch, Seneca, Epictetus, Philo, and others.

"In the Vishnu Purana, an ancient Brahminic

Scripture, we read: 'The earth is upheld by the veracity of those who have subdued their passions, and following righteousness, are never polluted with desire, covetousness, or wrath.' 'The Eternal makes not his abode in the heart of the man who covets another's goods, who injures any living creature, who utters harshness or untruth, who is proud in his iniquity, and his thoughts are evil.'

"'Kesava [a name of God] is most pleased with him who does good to others, who never utters calumny or falsehood, who never covets another's wife or another's goods, who does not smite or kill, who desires always the welfare of all creatures and of his own soul, whose pure heart taketh no pleasure in the imperfections of love and hatred. The man who conforms to the duties enjoined in the Scripture is he who best worships Vishnu [God]: there is no other way.'

"'The duties incumbent alike on all classes are the support of one's own household, marriage for the sake of offspring, tenderness toward all creatures, patience, humility, truth, purity, freedom from envy, from repining, from avarice, from detraction.'

"'Know that man to be the true worshiper of Vishnu, who, looking upon gold in secret, holds another's wealth but as grass, and directs all his thoughts to the Lord.' 'The Brahmin must look upon the jewels of another as if they were but pebbles.'"

17

HEBREW MONOTHEISM.

Hebrewism, whence the Christian religion is more directly derived, is but a contraction of Egyptian Cosmic Mythology; and here, as elsewhere, did those Israelitish seers and sages, prophets and teachers, strive to embody in their worship the Monotheistic idea. They discovered the natural tendency of the masses was to the sensuous; they would lift up into the spiritual of centralization. They did *not* deny the religious naturalness of Polytheism; in fact they acknowledged it in their efforts to establish the supremacy of Jehovah over other gods. "Thou shalt have no other gods before me," was the order of the great I AM of the Hebrews. Though their Jehovah was revealed to them representatively by angels, and indicated directly His selfish policies circumscribed to Israel alone — thus proving His personal priesthood — yet His devotees, as all other worshipers did and do, attributed to Him unlimited capacities. Thus, in the personal they opened up ideally toward the infinitely impersonal. He was revered as Creator, Ruler, and Lord. What is this but a sublime Monotheism?

Jesus, of the New Testament of the Lord, recognized the Monotheistic idea, and made it his cardinal rallying point. His Father was his infinite of aspiration. The angels who ministered to him were but messengers of his Father. What a terse definition from the interior man! "God is a spirit, and they that worship Him must worship Him in spirit and in

truth." The Pauline disciples of the Nazarene continued the same teachings concerning God, " in whom
we live, and move, and have our being; " and John,
the beloved, and exponent of apostolic affection, added
a newer beauty still to the ideal: "God is love, and he
that dwelleth in love dwelleth in God and God in him."
But here, too, is the recognition of the Polytheistic
accompaniments of Monotheism. Spirits, angels,
and archangels, are held in obeyance as ministrants.
Angels in the desert, in Gethsemane, at the crucifixion,
at the resurrection, were to Jesus the agencies of his
Father's will, and through his love and obedience to
them did he "worship the Father in spirit and in
truth." Angels, too, were the Apostles' guards and
guides, " sent to them who shall be heirs of salvation,"
but ever recognized as subordinate to the Lord of all,
" who is above all, and in all."

BLENDING DEIFIC IDEAS.

Hastily scanning the historic religions, nothing is
plainer than that Monotheism and Polytheism have
been parallel — have, in fact, been blended. It certainly is in accordance with the structure of the
universe, and of man, the transcript thereof. Everything in the external world is diverse, multiform,
variegated — philosophically Polytheistic. Man is all
this, infinitely changing in action and attribute, a unity
in diversity. Through all runs a central life, one great
soul, one heart-beat, one infinite law of love. Polytheism is but the outgrowth of Monotheism — its

eternal manifestation and its ministration to a beautiful necessity.

And that beautiful necessity is the transcendent law of progress. As says Theodore Tilton, in his *Golden Age*, comparing the "Old and New Religions:"

"The world is growing better, not worse. The past is dim in comparison with the brighter present. The future will eclipse both. Who can guess the glories of the golden age! Oh, to have remained unborn until the coming time — until the latest generation of mankind! But better *this* day than Plato's. The world now has a thousand sweets for the human soul which were never tasted by the patriarchs and prophets. And chief among all the reasons why one should prefer to live in the nineteenth century, rather than to have heard the harp-strings of David, or to have worshiped in the temple of Solomon, is the sublime fact that the world has a new religion to take the place of the old — a religion which lifts from our mortal life the overhanging clouds of a wrathful future — a religion by which death is stripped of its terrors and reclothed with sweet delights — a religion by which human hearts are taught to banish hatreds and to cherish love — a religion which shows God with a beckoning finger instead of a red right hand — a religion whose teacher says to the erring sons of men, 'I will not accuse you to the Father' — a religion which opens wide the gates of heaven, and proclaims to all mankind, 'Whosoever will, let him come!'

"The greatest achievement of the human intellect

throughout the whole course of human history is that triumph of faith which, against the traditions of the ages, has substituted for the flame-lit scowl of an angry Jupiter the ineffable benignity of our Father's face."

RELIGIOUS MISTAKE.

Human nature educationally oscillates from Polytheism to Monotheism, and *vice versa*. The inter-relation of the two does not seem to have been continuously recognized. Hence the profane extremism or the coldness of the devotee. The Polytheistic corresponds with affection; the Monotheistic with mental confidence. The world is now swinging from the Monotheistic to the Polytheistic, almost losing sight of the former in its joyful discovery of so "great a cloud of witnesses." Hence the theological chaos.

We would not for worlds lessen the value of the Polytheistic idea, but we are sure, from years of experience and observation, that this *alone* fails to inspire reverence and devotion. Are not the prevailing profanities largely traceable to this loss in the soul — the loss of the Monotheistic centrality of faith and deific communion? But the Polytheistic has the warmth of love, and incites us to the first Great Cause where the soul can rest. Those of us who have been schooled in angel ministry, who have been ushered into their presence, heard their bosoms throb on ours, felt the breathings of their inspirations, have learned this great truth: That our angels are constantly devising ways and means, direct or indirect, whereby to benefit us.

When an earth-cry of sorrow trembles up to the spirit realm, some loving angel bounds in response, perhaps in silence, and immediately finds some one who can help.   It may be to influence a man to draw a load of wood to a fireless sick home, or a bag of flour to hungry children, or a garment to a shivering stranger, or a loving word to a starved and forlorn heart.

Is it not a privileged duty and joy to pray to the angels, the same as we do to each other in every-day needs? to come often into the chamber of inner communion with them? The more frequent such prayer, with the object of discharging all practical responsibilities, the closer are we embosomed by the life of faith in their great world of love, growing us in their intellectual and moral images of character.

This Polytheistic worship, when centralized in soul to the recognition and embodiment of principles, is inductive — more interiorly — to aspiration after the essentially spiritual — the Impersonal of the Personal. Every mind, clothed according to grade of affectional intelligence, is conscious of a HOLY PRESENCE everywhere, of immeasurable love above and within us, of a divinity that is shaping all events, and that this divinity is cognate with natural law, developing us into the likeness of the ingermed beauty. The spiritual mind sees and feels design, intelligence, affection, Providence, and thence a worship in beneficent use, in rocks, waters, vegetations, animals, humanities, resting at length in the absolute of knowledge that this Inner Soul, whom we call God, is not a blind law, but a causative Wisdom, an *esse* of Love, binding all to agree, teaching us that when we are inspired by the beauty that flashes all around us, we are inspired of God; when we love justice and practice it, we are justified in God; when we sun our souls in the sweet lovelight of a brother or sister, or a child, we are communing with God; when we welcome a holy angel, we welcome God; when we forgive those who trespass against us, we understand God's forgiving love; when we love the good, the beautiful, and true, God is opening to us the gates of heaven. To lie low and feel humble and still, to sense sweetness in the hearts of all things; to enter deeper and deeper into the Soul of souls; to love all, to bless all, this is finding God; this is the Emanuel; this is God translated and translating into our inner life.

> " The song of life the atom sings,
>   Is one with that by angels sung;
>   For atoms form the finest strings,
>   With which the grandest harp is strung.
> And what are angels more than atoms strung
> To give the harmonies diviner tongue?
>
> " Divinest harmonics that fill
>   And permeate the boundless whole;
>   And which, like falling dews, distill
>   In softest music on the soul;
> While souls attuned to catch the grand refrain,
> In soul responses echo back the strain.
>
> " And thus life's anthem onward floats,
>   In ceaseless strains of melody;
>   While seeming discords swell the notes
>   Of that unbroken harmony
> Which sweeps the strings of God's eternal lyre,
> In each succeeding sphere an octave higher. "
>   —*Geo. Kates.*

CHAPTER XI.

RUSKIN, in his "Ethics of Dust," says: "For the ounce of slime which we had for political economy of competition, we have by political economy of co-operation, a sapphire, an opal, and a diamond, set in the midst of a star of snow."

A pharisaical spirit reveals a low plane of bigotry allied with both worlds. If any people are most *lamentably* obsessed, it is those who cherish such a spirit. The sarcastic thrust of the fatalistic author of "Whatever is, is Right," applies:

"There is a great deal of common sense in these obsessing 'devils,' as they are called. They have dropped the airs of self-righteousness themselves, and are making others do the same. They are better educated in spiritual things than the man is who feels holy himself, and says, 'In the name of God I command you devils to depart.' * * *

"Let us, in our feeble spiritual development, be truthful to the spirit obsessing, and not say to him: Come up from the darkness you are in, to the light that we are in; but rather let us be conscious of our own condition, and say to the spirit, Take our hands, and lead us from the darkness that surrounds us, to

the light that you possess. Let us remember it is
folly to try to cast out a mote from the spirit's eye,
when we have a beam in our own. Meet an obsessing
spirit in the clouds of self-righteousness, and he will
act very bad, and do much mischief, and befoul us;
meet him on a platform of common sense and reason,
and he will meet us as a man. Take off the airs and
phantoms of self-superiority in religion and spiritual
goodness, and obsession will cease forever."

How true it is that good people never brag of their
piety; they are modest and unpretentious. And those
who put on airs of superexcellence are ever broken
in upon at the vulnerable points.

THE POOR INDIAN'S HOPE.

And what if even the poor Indians, whom the
"pale faces" are pushing into their Pacific graves,
prove themselves braver in death, and after death
"returning good for the evil we do them"—what if
they are nearer the Christ-life than their murdering
Christian brethren?

Henry B. Whipple, Bishop of Minnesota, one of
the strongest and best friends the poor red-men have,
relates a circumstance, of his knowledge, illustrative
of the Indian character: "Among the Indians imprisoned in connection with the horrible Minnesota mas-
sacre of 1862, was a distinguished Indian who was
visited in prison by a gentleman who was a physician.
The Indian, being desirous of knowing a little of the
probable fate that was before him, asked the physician

what he thought the Government would do with him.
The physician, apprehending his case was a hopeless
one, hesitated to answer the inquiry. The Indian
repeated his question, when the doctor said to the
Indian, calling him by name, ' I fear they will hang
you.' The Indian dropped his eyes a moment to the
floor, then raised them, looked steadily at the doctor
and calmly remarked: ' Well, I don't care; I am not
afraid to die; when I go to the spirit world, I will go
up to the Great Spirit, and look Him right in the face,
and tell Him of the multiplied wrongs and cruelties
inflicted on His red children by the white man, and
He won't scold me much."

SPIRITS MAY BE BETTER THAN THEY SEEM.

Very proper people infer, because a spirit produces
contortions of the medium's muscles, or causes a
medium to dance, run or pound himself and others,
that they are evil. It only shows their ignorance
of magnetic laws and conditions. Such activity may
be essential to better control and health. We know
of a case where an Indian spirit made a medium run
around a house three times with hot speed ere he
could be allowed to lay hands on a sick child. The
magnetic force, then powerful, was effectual in healing. The whirl of the Dervishes, the dancing of the
Shakers, the muscular trembling of the Quakers, the
pounding of the Flagellettes, are inductive to magnetic sphericity with such souls and better spiritual
influx.

Nor is it a criterion of evil design because of blundering in the communication. There are ignorant spirits who experiment their way into knowledge by an effort at revealing themselves, and of course through imperfect media, at first make a poor headway. Be patient; time will develop wonderful things.

Fanny Green McDougal, relating one of her visions to *Brittan's Quarterly Journal*, speaks of a "class of spirits that have been operatives in the cotton-mills of England. They have lived in such a state of deformity and dwarfhood that they could no more conceive of the duties and rights of a free human soul than they could conceive themselves possessed of a royal pomp and power. They must change their state and come into better material conditions before they can progress spiritually. After a while they may have an ideal emigration to America, or something equivalent. Then they will have the idea of better wages, and more time for self-improvement."

"But they know, at least, that they are in the Spirit World," I ventured to say; "and if so, all these fantasms must appear the height of absurdity. Is it the office of wise and good spirits to cherish these illusions? Nay, is it consistent with a strict regard for truth?"

"I answer thy last question first, because it is often asked, and has never yet received the full and broad answer which its importance demands. It is not so much literal fact as the spirit of things that constitutes truth or falsehood. How should it affect science

to know if Newton founded his theory on the fall of
one or two apples? The principle involved is the only
important thing about it. And precisely in this way
have spirits been accused of lying, when they have
given as much of truth as could be understood or
accepted. It is conceded by all liberal moralists that
the intention to deceive constitutes the lie. By this
rule you will find that intelligent spirits are never
guilty of the imputed wrong. And yet the points of
view are so different between the giver and receiver of
instruction, that occasional misconstructions are not
only probable, but sometimes inevitable.

* * * * * *

"Always try the testimony of spirits as you would
any other testimony, by itself. Never surrender your
reason, your freedom, your individuality, to any spirit
in the body or out. These are your own, and there is
no power, finite or infinite, that has any right to
infringe them.

"There may be a few exceptions to this in some
very peculiar cases and periods of development. But
in the main the rule holds good; and if it were
adhered to, there would be fewer silly and ridicu-
lous things done in the name of spirits than are now
witnessed."

There is much truth in this vision of our gifted
author. The fault may be often our own, more than
the spirit's. Our blundering confuses their manifestation. Looking through our soiled glasses—mental-
ity—daubed with ignorance and filthy habits, how can

spirits then appear to us in their beautiful aspects? Put the glasses in order, and see how the great light will come in.

Our physical condition, from transmitted and educated habits, deflecting to the spiritual relationally, develops a corresponding grade of manifestations, the most tangible of which is the materialization of a spiritual body. The process is doubtless analogous with natural gestation and birth—the sexual and every other organ of the body contributing its ethereal share, which, aggregated together, presents to the natural eye a visible creation—a spirit *in persona* identically revealed. If, then, these magnetically procreative organs are perverted or befouled in unnatural relations, and so functionally diseased—thus projecting clouded and poisoning exhalations upon the brain and thence affecting the mind—the *manifest* spiritual body to the observer will be in texture and appearance a *dark veil* of that spirit, while the *spirit* itself may be clear and bright as the celestial morning in heaven. As to the good part thus revealed we must be our own judges, dating from the life *we live*, and careful analysis of the instructions which such spirits impart.

So far as we now know, it is safe to conclude, if the presence of a spirit, whether materialized or not, leaves us in moral abandon and gloom, by exchange of spheres, that such spirit is in a starved condition, and needs our help. Says Jung Stilling: "When a departed spirit is tranquil in its mind, its touch is felt to be like the softness of a cool air—exactly as when the electric fluid is poured upon any particular part of the body. The spirit's body is therefore entirely in the power of the mind, and it forms itself inwardly and outwardly according to the imagination and the inward propensities."

Over brain work in earth life, passional excess, nervous excitements and shocks, unbalanced sympathies, habitual jealousies, mismated relations, are among the causes of depletion, ever warping and injuring the gestative process of spiritual embodiment. A spirit so reduced must be in a most deplorable condition, being obliged to procure help mediumistically, preying upon a medium with a ravenous thirst and educing the madness we often observe when so controlled. It is no longer a wonder why certain media have been tempted! A reliable friend of ours, who was present as witness, states that a poor, famished spirit, mad and furious, made various attempts to procure relief in a circle. Prayer, singing, advising, eating, and other expedients were tried, but failed. At length the spirit said, through the medium, " Pile up your hands alternately one upon the other." They did so, and the spirit sipped from that new voltaic battery and obtained strength, and afterwards by other aids progressed into beautiful balance.

In one of our (Sen. Editor's) visions, we saw a banquet in the spirit world. Scores of spirits were seated around a table loaded with a rich variety of food and drink; all enjoying the feast with great hilarity, amid joke and vivacity, thus generating a healthful and gestative atmosphere. At one end of the table sat a famished woman, who for years had tried in the spirit world to get relief, and at last, by the kind offices of the friends we saw, gradually recuperated by this magnetic imbibation. Waking from the vision, the conviction was strong upon our mind, that such methods of cure are also practical in earth life. Spirits returning see that we need fun and frolic; they induce all manner of healthful amusement; they inspire departure from dead customs and habits. Let us not interpret their electric activities as unworthy of such guardianship.

Years agone, more especially when the priesthood held sway over the minds of the masses, and science was circumscribed to the inspection of the few, it was an easy matter for the clergy, by means of the cross or bible or prayers to exorcise an obsessing or unhappy spirit,—that was troubled perhaps as to where lay its earthly bones,—or produce a timely suspension of disturbances, because all this corresponded with the superstitious educations of such spirits who believed the clergy were God-appointed, and their rites were sacred; but, of course, such interference wrought no real change or improvement, no more than a vicious child is reformed when its whims are indulged by an unwise parent. These days the clerical office no longer hides human weaknesses and follies, and those serving here are generally shorn of every power to compete with spirit agency, because of their pampered preju-

dices and habitually spiritual imbecility, not being
informed nor willing to inform themselves. Spirits
know this in our nineteenth century, and are learning by experiences most trying that there are no
proxy methods by which to eradicate their troubles,
no ecclesiastic, royal road to heaven, no priest or
church, or sacred book, or holy shrine, that has power
to compensate for the derelictions of the earth-life.

A palliating truth is to be considered. A large percentage of mental suffering, irrespective of worlds, is
conventional and abnormal. A superstitious or sectarian spirit, pure in heart, may therefore appear
unhappy, but the moment, as by a flash of light, this
psychic influence fades away, its mind is illuminated
with angelic joy. Wherever the central affections
were good, it is thus easy for the external character
to right itself. So, much of the darkness cast upon
us from the spirit side is mere appearance. This
fact in spirit science is illustrated in the law of identi-
fication. The experiences of spirits are like our own
in the chemistries of life. Conditionally we can return
to other days. Imagination at play, we relive the joys
or sorrows of the past. By the law of materialization,
emotions generate their corresponding spheres, and
these by an innate instinct organically shape themselves, analogous with a crystalizing process, to appear
to the medium what that spirit once was in earth-life—
appear just as the feeling is at the time of emotional
retrospection.

Professor E. Whipple truly says: "People, by the

corrupting nature of education and impression are so
apt to associate their dear ones out of the material
form with the wo-begone condition of matters here,
that it renders it very difficult for them to overcome
the advantage that these impressions give to a false
class of spirits (not unfortunate) against any attempt
that they may make to reach us. When it shall be
accepted that ours is an imposed-upon condition of
being — that everybody is more or less unnatural, by
constraint and misdirection, having their origin in the
unseen — the scale will turn in favor of those who love
us. For the difficulty now is in man's ignorance of the
real condition of things. For man is conscious of
being unnatural without directly suspecting the cause,
which cannot be a result from himself; for whatever
that should be, would be natural. Hence our condition here, under the circumstances, may not be inaptly
compared to a steel bow, the opposite ends of which
are drawn toward each other by a strong cord. This
sundered, the bow assumes its natural condition. So,
at death, the soul — out of its natural, lovable element here, by the network of constraint thrown about
it and the direct oppression of subtle spirits — when
released from these oppressions, is at once itself. Man,
go into your own independent soul, and spirits can
find you as easy as bees can find flowers."

Let us beware how we throw the coverlid of our
drowsiness over the spirit watchers of our voluptuous
slumbers; lest we

18

" Check and chide
The ærial angels, as they float about us
With robes of a so-called wisdom, till they grow
The same tame slaves to custom and the world."

The return of a spirit quickens into life the unbalanced remains of old habits; and by such activity that
spirit may afterwards make a new progress, *when the
mediumistic agency is orderly in truth and goodness.*
It is the same as it is in magnetic healing. The stirring of the deadening disease by a healthful manipulation till the patient for the time feels worse, is a sign
of constitutional vitality—that nature is thus trying to
restore itself.

Judge Edmonds relates a case like this: " I knew
a man—a noble man by nature—a graduate, a soldier
in the revolution, a general in the army of 1812—who
imbibed a love for liquor. It was the fashion then.
The habit grew upon him. He finally died of 'delirium tremens.' This army general had a son highly
mediumistic, whom the parent influenced more or less.
Thus returning to the more material plane with its
lingering memories and tendencies to previous habits,
he influenced the son to imbibe the poisoned draught.
The habit was growing; the son was conscious of it
and tried to stop; he prayed for help; and yet, with
a prayer on his lips, he would pour down the gin. He
would resolve to go by a liquor-house, and yet, moved
by a mighty impulse, would go straight into it. He
said to himself, '*I cannot stop!*' He was almost in
despair. Finally, with a determined struggle—and
divine reliance upon God and angels for help—he

broke the spell. The appetite—the *desire*—was gone
in a moment, and has not returned for years. This
general has been in the spirit-world thirty years. This
son, by his will-power and victory, accomplished a
double result—saving himself and parent in the
spirit-world. A further result was the uniting con-
jugially of those whom habit had separated, into
perfect relationship of love and harmony."

SPIRITS OBSESSED BY THEIR MEDIA!

As the spirit of a man interblends with his body,
the forces of each correlated, so are spirits and the
influences of their world united with mortals and
their world of interests. Often is a spirit, magnetically inhabiting the body and mind of its medium,
affectionally represented in every part by the copart-
nership of spheres, till the emotions of one transmits
its force to the other, like two responsive, musical
chords. As spirits are just as dependent upon mortals for support as mortals upon spirits, the latter can
be as readily reached by the former as *vice versa*.
For aught we know, the effect of spirit-intercourse
with those of earth-life that are positive to them, may
cast a dark shadow there. They often aver that a
descent into certain atmospheres here is more painful
and repellant than death; but they cheerfully do it
from sympathy for our benighted conditions; and in
our joy thus awakened they at last find their heaven.
It is like a philanthropist entering the haunts of
moral pestilence where he must suffer to rescue the

lost.   Spirits often have to insulate themselves by
great force of will against the malaria of these magnetisms; but the peril is only superficial to such as
are principled in loves of truth and goodness.   Where
a spirit is not thus interiorly illuminated, and is
attracted back to earth-life, even with the good motive
of blessing suffering mortals, if negative—as such a
condition evolves—it is liable to obsession from the
unbalanced media with which it may affiliate; and
who can reasonably deny that such are tortured, that
multitudes of such are terribly crucified?   It makes
no difference whether a spirit is an inhabitant of the
physical or spirit-world; the effects of starvation are
the same, educing a ravenous appetite of the inner
affections.   So tyrants prey upon inharmonious spirits,
obsessing them to do their bidding and serve their
insatiable purposes to gain power.   Let us be careful
how we charge spirits of any grade with criminality,
lest sin may lie at the very door of our own hearts!
Luther Colby related to us a case of a spirit, called
by a medium to perform the "physical manifestations," with a high and noble object; but when the
league was formed between them, and the spirit by
the force of the medium's magnetism was compelled
to follow him and participate associatively with all
his debaucheries, the spirit seriously protested against
such demoralization, accusing him of enclosing its
mental sphere with a dark, mephitic effluvia.   The
history of disorderly mediumship from the spirit-side
remains yet to be written, when we may have poor

reasons for charging the heavens with uncleanness, as we inspect the sad effect of our social perversities upon the angel-world. How extensive and solemn, then, are our responsibilities! If our lives are right, so are spirits also blessed. If we hunger and thirst after righteousness, however ignorant or unfortunate we may be, it is a prayer that the holy spirits answer in beneficence. And when we are thus made strong we should be willing to bless other spirits of a lower grade, whether in or out of the earthly tabernacle. To enlighten and save is the object of exchange between the two worlds. It is often a great burden to take on the dark spheres of unhappy spirits; but this relieves them, if we are faithful, just the same as in the healing art by laying on of hands, when the healer receives the diseased sphere and scatters it, and gives one of magnetic health in exchange; as was said of the Nazarene—"Himself took our diseases and bear our sicknesses. * * With his stripes we are healed." The prerequisite, then, to success with an unregenerate spirit, is a fearless moral courage on our part—sound physical health—a positive will—a forgiving and loving disposition. In short, we ourselves must be regenerated from all groveling desires. Then, in casting out, shall we be able to save both medium and spirit, and so prevent an obsession in another quarter.

THE SHAKERS.

The Shakers, though abstemious in all their ways, living the most self-denying life, after the pattern of the Essenians, passed through the same ordeal preparatory to higher influx from angels. Elder F. W. Evans, writing us says: "That Spiritualism began and went out from this order, you are well aware, I suppose. During the seven years from about 1842 to 1849, we did certainly have some experience in 'obsession,' and every other form and phase of inter-mundane and super-spiritual communication."

This revered brother and lecturer, contrasting an incongruous Spiritualism with celibate life, speaks thus of the remedy for the usual glutted and obsessional habits of society as it now is: "It is my present theology that in unfallen worlds, Shaker (or resurrection) organizations exist in numbers equal to the populative emergency (as wheat in the farmers' granaries reserved for other uses than seed); there being in them none of the destructive agencies which hold population in check on this globe, such as perverted nutrition and generation — 'eating and drinking, marrying and giving in marriage,' not for use, but lust; engendering all forms of evil; physical diseases, wars, and fightings — murder of adults, and 'murder of the innocents' in all stages of embryonic existence —'the social evil' (now so hellishly popular); slavery, poverty, famines, monopoly, usury, aristocracy, doctors, lawyers, priests and mediums, 'living upon the sins of God's people;' the doctors administering poisons to keep patients sick; 'the priests preaching for hire, and the mediums divining for money.'"

A JUST CHARITY.

Our pity, rather than our condemnation, should go out to those who are obsessed, when they perform acts that cause us to blush. Our pharisaical criticism will only augment the difficulty. When we understand the causes, and are able to meet them with saving influences to all concerned, then are we qualified to judge as to merit or demerit of character. It is a well-known law in psychologizing, that the subject tastes, feels, thinks, and acts as the operator does; and that when the operator, during the magnetic sleep, commands the subject to do a certain thing, that subject, when awake, feels that the act must be performed. That command may be given in silence, but it will, of course, be just as imperative.

How easy, then, for a mischievous spirit to educe strange manifestations of character in its unwary medium, which would be scorned in a normal condition of mind. But this does not remove the personal responsibility of the medium. Even in the unconscious trance the soul is most wakeful; it is ever the god of the body, holding itself absolutely responsible for all the deeds done by or in the body, keeping record of all, whether automatic or volitionary. And how elevating if the psychic control to which the soul consents be morally wise; how ennobling if thus the soul regenerates the communicating spirit, seeking light in mediumship — if thereby both are made wiser and better.

REGENERATION IN SPIRIT LIFE.

Robert Dale Owen, in his "Debatable Land," happily says: "There is repentance there as here. There
is restless regret and sorrow for grave sins committed
while here. There is anxious desire for pardon from
those whom the spirit wronged during earth life. In
other words, the natural effects of evil doing follow us
to our next phase of life; and in that phase of life, as
in the present, we amend, and attain to better things
by virtue of repentance.

"In this the mode of moral progression after death
is similar, which alone avails on earth. 'Repent!'
was Christ's first public exhortation. To the 'spirits
in prison' on the other side — spirits not yet released
from earthly bondage and earthly remorse — the same
exhortation, it would seem, is appropriate still."

Samuel Benjamin Walthers, A. D. 1730, narrates in
his interesting work entitled "Monthly Discourses on
the World of Spirits," that about 1715, Christian,
Duke of Saxe Eisenberg, was reposing upon his couch
at noon, when some one knocked at the door, and, as
was his custom, he answered, "Come in!" on which
a female figure representing Anna, daughter of one of
the Electors of Saxony, entered, attired in an ancient
princely robe. The spirit identified herself as the wife
John Casimer, Duke of Saxe Coburg, and that they
both had been in the spirit world above a hundred
years. She then informed Christian that in the earth-
life her husband was jealous of her on account of her

frequent conversation with a cavalier in private upon
religious matters. Although she established her innocence, he was unrelenting. She entreated reconciliation
on her death bed, but he was stubborn and hateful.
She was in a state of blessedness, but not at full rest
because of her husband. He confessed his guilt in
prayer, but, not being yet reconciled, continued all this
while in "cold and darkness." Having stated these
facts, the spirit then said it was in the power of
Christian to reconcile them. After repeated evidence
of the good intent of the spirit, through other visita-
tions bearing upon the request, and committing
himself to long meditation and prayer, he consented
to act as mediator according to the heavenly order.
A night was set — not day, for she averred her husband, because of his spiritual condition, could not
appear in the light. They both came. He heard their
full statement, he being appointed umpire. He decided
in her favor. Then joined their hands and pronounced
a blessing in the name of God. They all three sung
a hymn, after which they vanished out of sight,
rejoicing together at the reconciliation.

At the twenty-third Anniversary of the advent of
Modern Spiritualism, held in Boston, March 31st,
Lizzie Doten delivered one of her soul-breathing poems,
founded upon this incident related by Richter, the
German writer:

"The hero of the tale forsook his wife — a patient,
loving woman whom he had most cruelly misunder-
stood. After years of absence he returned to his home

19

and upon inquiring for her he was directed to her grave. He visited it in the clear moonlight of a summer's night; and as he stood beside it he felt that his repentance had come too late. Turning sorrowfully away he retraced his steps to the inn. On re-entering it he found there a wandering minstrel — a woman — who sang a sad song, accompanying herself with the music of a harp; and the burden of her song was: 'Gone is gone, and dead is dead!' The utter hopelessness of these words filled his soul with anguish. 'Oh,' he exclaimed, 'thou loved one! patient and long-suffering, would that I could call thee back again, not to forgive me — oh no! — but rather that I might have the consolation of suffering for thy sake, and of showing thee by my repentance how differently I would conduct toward thee now!'"

Such is the natural feeling and plea of the soul when conscious of its unkind suspicion and treatment of a loved one. If not here, it must there awaken to pain of repentance that would fain return the slighted hours and the beloved friend. How differently then would we behave! how true our love! But can it be? Can we ever outgrow the regrets of such recollections? We ask the serious question in tears, looking up to the great angels for an answer. Is there a Lethean stream? Is there a forgiveness that will make all earth's clouds great mountains of gold whereon our souls can be transfigured into the glory of virtue? Ask of Love, come to its heart, perform good deeds to the living,

and then is not the poem from our risen sister, Achsa
W. Sprague, realized?

> " Evermore Love's quickening breath
>   Calls the living soul from death;
>   And the resurrection's power
>   Comes to every dying hour.
>   When the soul, with vision clear,
>   Learns that heaven is always near,
>   Never more shall it be said,
> ' Gone is gone, and dead is dead!'"

It is something to think of, those whom we have
blest are our loving guardians, and whom we have
wronged are just as near, kindling the fire within to
consume the guilt, resting not until justice is done by
reconciliation.   The trespass against the divine of
human nature ties the injured to us as accusing spirits.
Strike the steel and it is polarized.   Even a suspicion
unconfessed and unreconciled may mar the serenity of
the parties for long, suffering years   The tender
angels grieve over the least stain, and rest not until it
is obliterated.

SPIRITUAL VESTURES.

When in order of life and habit, a spirit, in or out
of the earthly body, is re-clothing itself with purer
and finer elements, progressively, as Anna Blackwell
says: " While a spirit remains ignorant and impure,
its *périsprit* [the permanent fluidic body which is the
inseparable envelope of spirit, or spiritual body,] composed of fluidic particles corresponding to its state, and

magnetically attracted by that state, is almost as dense
and gross as a material body; but as it progresses in
knowledge and purity it attracts to its *périsprit* fluidic
particles of a progressively finer and more ethereal
order, and the more etherealized *périsprit*, in its turn,
material elements of a higher and less heavy quality;
the material bodies become gradually more and more
fluidic, until they attain to states of ethereality so
refined as practically to release it from the limitations
of space and time."

The comparative darkness attending certain spirits
for a long period in the land of souls, is only the reflex
action of their own spiritual states. They generate
the mist that dims their vision. The malicious and
depraved of this, carrying their hells with them, enter
the hells or lower spheres of the spirit-life. Their
affections centered upon earth and earthly things, by
an inexorable law of their being they are mentally and
psychologically imprisoned for a time near the surface
of this planet. As fish to water, bird to air, so the
earthly minded to the grosser strata and aural circles
belting the earth, till through aspiration, unfoldment,
and refinement, they become prepared to traverse the
starry spaces of the higher heavens.

The New Testament scriptures inform us that Jesus,
after being put to " death in the flesh, but quickened
by the spirit, preached to the *spirits* in prison."
Peter further speaks of the " gospel being preached to
them that are *dead*." The fact of such preaching
implies a moral benefit derived therefrom.

CHAPTER XII.

The author of Euthanasy has finely said: "In my character there are the effects of Paul's journey to Damascus, and the meeting of King John and the Barons at Runneymede. There is in my soul the seriousness of the many conflicts, famines and sorrows of early English times. And of my enthusiasm, some of the warmth is from fiery words that thrilled my forefathers in the days of the reformation."

Jean Reynaud well says, "Each one of us carries in his actual form and organism the secret history of his anterior emotions; so accurately, that spiritual eyes, penetrating to the depths of our being, see at a glance all that we *have* been in all that we *are*."

"The stars in their courses sing!" Verily, for they impinge against resisting media as they revolve and sweep through the awful void. Being of different sizes, texture, tension, and revolution, the sounds are myriad, commingling into the eternal symphony that enchants the homes of the immortals.

And who shall confront our ancient brethren, who averred that the stars rule us; that here is demarked our destiny? The soil we tread upon affects us; the trees over our heads engrave their very foliage on our brains; the kisses of the grassy tips thrill us through from palms of feet to dome of thought; the beauty of flowers enchants us, and their fragrances soften our natures; the old gray rocks, as we lay our heads there, gird us to strength; the winds remove our fevers; the sunbeams bloom us in soul as they do all the land-scapes; the snows whiten our ideas as they do our locks. Where is the boundary to this elemental rela-tionship and susceptibility to inspiration? If a slight wave of water or zephyr moves us so, how much more must a great world in space, concentrating in us its mighty battery of life! Think not that these nightly stars, that seem twinkling in a cerulean arch, are meant only for guidance in the dark or poesy's flame of aspiration. As they mirror themselves, cold and weird, in the focus of our souls, they distill there the very nature of all their qualities, and affiliate us for-ever so with the intelligent beings peopling their seas and island continents, whom we shall yet greet as we veer upward unfolding into their immortal beatitudes.

What a sublime truth bursts upon us here! Our relations with the universe are such, that, by this reg-istry, we live all the past in the present. The (French) author of "Lumen" has philosophically elaborated this fact; and prior to this the author of "The Earth and Stars" presents the same chain of reasoning:

"The universe encloses the pictures of the past, like an indestructible and incorruptible record con-taining the purest and clearest truth. * * As thun-der and lightning are in reality simultaneous, but in

the storm the distant thunder follows at the interval
of some minutes after the flash; so, in like manner,
according to our ideas, the pictures of every occurrence propagate themselves into the distant ether,
upon the wings of the ray of light; and, although
they become weaker and smaller, yet, in immeasurable
distance, they still have color and form; and as every
thing possessing color and form is visible, so must
these pictures also be said to be visible, however
impossible it may be for the human eye to perceive
them with the hitherto discovered optical apparatus.
Thus that record which spreads itself out further and
further in the universe, by the vibration of the light,
really and actually exists and is visible, but to eyes
more powerful than those of man."

The same author makes an astronomical calculation
by which a spiritual intelligence might actually see
enacted all the events of the past. He starts from the
basis of the velocity of light that travels—as discovered by eclipses—at the rate of two hundred and
thirty-seven thousand miles in a second. Having
ascertained the distances of the planets and fixed
stars, he shows that a star of the first magnitude will
send its light to our earth in from three to twelve years;
of the second magnitude, in twenty years; of the
third, in thirty years; of the fourth, in forty-five
years; of the fifth, in sixty-six years; of the sixth, in
ninety-six years; of the seventh, in one hundred and
eighty years. On the calculation of Strüve, who
maintains that a star of the twelfth magnitude is

twenty-three thousand billions of miles off, our author
shows it will take a ray of light from such a star four
thousand years to reach our earth.   According to
this, the light of a star of the twelfth magnitude—
only perceptible by a very good telescope—"has, at
the time it meets our eye, already left its star four
thousand years, and since that time has wandered on
its own course, unconnected with its origin." It is
plain that a ray of light meeting our eye is not sent
forth from the star at the same moment; consequently,
we do not see the star as it now is, but as it was when
its ray was emitted. Finding the time it takes for
light to pass from different worlds to our earth, this
author enables a spiritual observer, traveling with the
velocity of light itself, to witness and experience all
the events of the past that have occurred in human
history. If that observer were standing on the moon,
observing the light of our planet, he would not see it
as it is, but as it was five quarters of a second ago; if
standing on the sun he would see our planet as it was
eight minutes ago; on Jupiter, as it was fifty-two
minutes ago; on Uranus, two hours ago; on Vega
in Centaur, twelve years ago; on a star of the twelfth
magnitude, four thousand years ago, when Memphis
in Egypt was founded. "In the immeasurably great
number of fixed stars which are scattered about in
the universe, floating in ether at a distance of between
fifteen to twenty billions of miles from us, reckoning
backward any given number of years, doubtless a star
could be found which sees the past epochs of our earth

as if existing now, or so nearly corresponding to the time, that the observer need wait no long time to see its condition at the required moment. * * * It is not in contradiction with the laws of thought, that a man may travel to a star in a given time; and he may effect this, provided with so powerful a telescope as to be able to overcome every given distance, and every light and shadow in the object to be examined. * * With the aid of a knowledge of the position and distance of every given fixed star (to be attained by the study of astronomy), it will be possible to recall sensibly to our very eyes an actual and true represent-ation of every moment of history that has passed. If, for instance, we wish to see Luther before the council at Worms, we must transport ourselves in a second to any fixed star, from which the light requires about three hundred years (or so much more or less) in order to reach the earth. Thence the earth will appear in the same state, and with the same persons moving upon it as it actually was at the time of the Reforma-tion. * * * Let us imagine an observer, with infinite powers of vision, in a star of the twelfth mag-nitude. He would see the earth at this moment as it existed at the time of Abraham. Let us, moreover, imagine him moved forwards in the direction of our earth, with such speed, that in a short time (say in an hour) he comes to within a distance of a hundred millions of miles, being then as near to us as the sun is whence the earth is seen as it was eight minutes before; then before the eye of this observer the entire history of the world, from the time of Abraham to the present day, passes by in the space of an hour. * * * If we divide this hour into four thousand parts, so that about a second corresponds to each, he has seen the events of a whole year in a single second. They have passed before him with all the particulars, all the motions and positions of the persons occupied with the entire changing scenery, and he has lived through them all—every thing entire and unshortened, but only in the quickest succession—and one hour was for him crowded with quite as many events as the space of four thousand years upon the earth. If we give the observer power also to halt at pleasure in his path, as he is flying through the ether, he will be able to represent to himself, as rapidly as he pleases, that moment in the world's history which he wishes to observe at leisure; provided he remains at a distance when this moment of history appears to have just arrived, allowing for the time which the light consumes in traveling to the position of the observer."

Though some of these conclusions are based upon a supposed date, they are real prophesies of what will be in the beautiful hereafter. Accepting the deductive law as truthful, that other worlds than ours are peopled with progressive intelligencies, they must in time discover methods by which to communicate and observe the daily and hourly transactions of each star and planet with the facility that we now telegraph across the ocean, and so read, as already described, the histories of the indelible past. What a stupendous thought, and how solemn its moral import!

But we are not left to the tardy researches of materialistic scientists in the discovery of these truths. As with all other developments, mediumnistic intuitions, under the sweet guidance of the risen seers, have laid bare in the light the registry of life. By the delicate touch of magnetic spheres, of mind with matter, of sentient intelligence with unsentient motion of elements, crystallized or gaseous, we can read the psychological hieroglyphics of eternal events, and hear again the voices of the past in the dim sepulchres of the so-called dead. Seizing upon the magnetic threads that time is only weaving, that stretch from the object once touched with the immortal genius who, ages gone, stamped the imagery thereon, we can trace on and up to the mind-world of causation, whence may come to us correct statements of what was done under the sun.

Not long since an English company, under the corporate seal of the British government, sent out an expedition of discovery to the classic lands. After several years of toil and search they found the ancient site of the Temple of Diana, of Ephesus, under an alluvial deposit of twenty-two feet. They exhumed those marble columns and transferred them to the British Museum. Says a correspondent of the London *Times:* "The largest, weighing upward of eleven tons, is part of a drum of one of the *cælatæ columnæ* mentioned by Pliny — *i. e.* columns with figures sculptured on them, of which the temple has thirty-six.

Of this bold, striking innovation of Greek architecture there exists, it is believed, no other example except at Ephesus. The relief of this drum appears to represent an assemblage of deities, of whom the only one who can be positively identified is Mercury, the rest being draped female figures. On a stone from a pilaster, corresponding in dimensions to the sculptured drum, is a relief representing Hercules struggling with a draped female figure; and on another fragment of a drum are the lower halves of some seated and standing female figures. This sculpture is very bold and effective as a decoration, but wants the ineffable charm and freshness of the frieze of the Parthenon, while in masterly vigor of execution and dramatic force, it falls short of the frieze of the Mausoleum. It is careless and inexact in execution, and has the characteristics which we might expect to find in the Greek sculpture of the Macedonian period, when work was executed rapidly to gratify the vanity of kings, and when an Oriental love for mere mass rather than beauty of design had begun to affect both sculpture and architecture. Allowing for this first disappointment, I own that I gazed with a peculiar interest on these relics of those famous columns on which St. Paul must have gazed when he preached against them, but which local fanaticism, aided by local vested interests, preserved in all their splendor for three centuries after his coming."

What does that British Museum now contain? Simply those grand old columns, those pilasters, those dim and colossal images, resurrected as from the dead at the trumpet call of science? On those carved relics, living in their very fibres, and living there were they crumbled to dust, are the psychological imagery of the classic feasts, gladiatorial sports, moving columns of military victors, the faces of sceptered kings and emperors, the voices of orators, the song of musicians commemorating the national battles, the bloody sacrifices of priests, the groans of the prisoner, the shrieks of the insane, the love and beauty of women, the jealousy and fierceness of sensuous tyrants, the prattle of childhood, the mystic rustle and alarming minstrelsy of the spiritual oracles that shaped the civilizations and religions of those ages, now reviving in fresher effulgence. All these are there, to be read, and heard, and revoiced by the seers of the Nineteenth century.

And so are we to-day writing our history for all time, to be read by us and generations coming. Every tread of our feet upon the ground leaves its magnetic imprint; every motion of our hand burns forever in the eternal light of its history; every heart pulse musicalizes itself in the great beating soul of the universe; every look of the eye stamps itself on the earth and bending sky; every thought that trembles in its convoluting brain is trembling still through all the heavens of inspecting angels.

"The air," says Professor Babbage, "is one vast library, on whose pages are forever written all that man has ever said or woman whispered."

We find in a recent number of the *London Times* a story for mothers, and as it contains a beautiful answer to some letters we have received, we give it entire: "On a December night, after the little brood were all abed, a mother sat thinking over what she had accomplished in the last year. To her it seemed to have been one of fruitless effort, broken and disjointed. She had done nothing but keep the house and family, and even this seemed to have been but indifferently done. Yearnings she had for something better, to be conscious of some unity of purpose, some weaving together of the life-threads so broken and single, some comfortable assurance of what was duty. That night in her dreams she was traversing a vast plain, where no trees were visible save those that skirted the distant horizon, with a wreath of golden clouds resting upon their tops. Before her, traveling toward that distant light, was a female with little children about her, sometimes in her arms, sometimes at her side; and as she journeyed on she busied herself caring for them. Now she soothed them when weary, now she taught them how to travel, and now she warned them of the pitfalls and stumbling blocks in the way. She talked to them of that golden light which she kept constantly in view, and toward which she seemed hastening with her little flock. But what was most remarkable, all unknown to her, on two golden clouds floating above her reposed two angels. Before each was a golden book and a pen of gold. One angel, with mild and loving eyes, peered constantly over the right shoulder, and the other over the left. They followed her from the rising to the setting of the sun; they watched every word, and look, and deed, no matter how trivial. When it was good the angel over the right shoulder, with a glad smile, wrote it down in his golden book; when evil, however slight, the angel over the left shoulder wrote it down in his book. He kept his sorrowful eyes upon her until he found penitence for the evil; then he dropped a tear upon his record and blotted it out, and both angels rejoiced. To the lookers-on it seemed that the traveler did little worthy of such careful record. Sometimes she did but bathe the weary feet of her children, yet that was recorded in the golden book; sometimes she did but wait patiently to lure back some little truant who had taken a step in the wrong direction, and that, too, was set down by the angel over the right. Sometimes, with her eyes fixed upon the golden horizon, she became so intent on her own progress as to let the little pilgrims at her side languish or stray; then the angel over the left shoulder wrote it down in his book, but followed her with sorrowing eyes seeking to blot it out; if, wishing to hasten on her journey, she left the little ones behind, that, too, the sorrowing angel recorded. The sympathies of the dreamer were warmly excited for the traveler, and with a beating heart she quickened her steps that she might overtake her, tell her what she had seen, entreat her to be watchful, faithful, and patient to the end of her life's work, for she had herself seen that its results would all be known when these golden books should be unclasped. Eager to warn her of this, she gently touched her. The traveler turned, and she recognized, or seemed to recognize, herself."

It may or may not be that angels keep a record like this; but it is certain that every impulse of life and deed is ineffaceably written on our immortal being to be inspected by and by.

Pressure upon the brain stops mental action. When it is removed, the last idea finding expression when the blow is received, will be uttered, even if months and years intervene.

Thus the mind holds all its pictures and thought-pulses, even though its media is obstructed; and those most active at death are most fresh and vigorous on waking to consciousness on the "other side," making life but one continuous Now — death but the hyphen that connects the two worlds. Is it not of some moral moment, then, when we are ushered into the embodied presence of immortals and hail the first dawn of celestial light, that our last hours be hallowed to holy communings? that our thoughts and words be as links of love holding close and strong in magnetic power with the "just made perfect?" that the mental aura our angels shall first sense with gratitude, and its voice sent back to identify us to earthly friends, trembling on our dying lips, shall correctly sign the plane of our life in the "beauty of holiness?"

J. O. Barrett's Works.

SPIRITUAL PILGRIM:

A BIOGRAPHY OF JAMES M. PEEBLES.

With beauty of style, the author has given full accounts of this celebrated writer and speaker, in all his travels; comprising facts of varied laws of mediumship, with a FINE LIKENESS of Mr. Peebles. Single copy, $1.50; Postage, 20 cts.

LOOKING BEYOND:

A souvenir of love to the bereft of every home — welcomed with joy for its sunny Philosophy. Single copy, 75 cts; Postage, 12 cts.

SOCIAL FREEDOM:

MARRIAGE AS IT IS AND AS IT SHOULD BE.

An analytical and beautiful treatise on the SOCIAL QUESTION, comprehending all the main issues, and proving that the highest freedom is compatible with the strictest virtue. Single copy, 25 cts; six copies, $1.20; twelve copies, $2.00.

SPIRITUAL HARP:

BY

J. O. BARRETT, J. M. PEEBLES, and E. H. BAILEY.

Popular all over the world, it is so full of beautiful words and inspiring melodies. Single copy, $2.00. Postage, 26 cts; six copies, $10.00; twelve copies, $19.00; Gilt, $12.50; Abridged, $11.00; Postage, 14 cts.

COLBY & RICH,

No. 9 MONTGOMERY PLACE,

BOSTON, MASS.

Modern Spiritualism.

By EPES SARGENT.

PLANCHETTE : THE DESPAIR OF SCIENCE.

Being a Full Account of Modern Spiritualism.

PRICE IN ILLUMINATED PAPER COVERS, $1; IN GREEN CLOTH, $1.25. POSTAGE, 16c.
A New Edition, just issued by ROBERTS BROTHERS, Boston.

This volume should be properly called "A History of Modern Spiritualism," for it is a thorough and careful survey of the whole subject of well-attested phenomena believed to be spiritual.

Prof. WM. CROOKES, F. R. S., of London, the celebrated chemist, whose scientific verifications of the spiritual phenomena are now creating such a sensation, writes, under date of April 17, 1874, —
"*Planchette* was the first book I read on Spiritualism, and it still remains in my opinion, the best work to place in the hands of the uninitiated."

GEO. WM. CURTIS, in HARPER's WEEKLY, says of it, —
"It is a copious and popular but faithful summary of the phenomena and theories. The ample knowledge and literary skill with which the subject is treated make this volume an indispensable manual to all who are attracted to this speculation, and it will be read with great interest by the skeptic as well as by the believer."

The Rev. Dr. BELLOWS, in the LIBERAL CHRISTIAN, says of it, —
"It sets forth many important considerations with regard to the philosophy of the mind, while its historical notices of the development of Spiritualism during the last twenty years give a more complete and impartial view of the phenomena in question than has thus far been presented to the public."

The New York Express says, —
"This is certainly one of the most startling works of our sensational age. It purports to give a duly authenticated narration of spiritual manifestations, which are beyond the bounds of credulity by any calm thinking reader; and yet the asserted facts are given with such an apparent truthfulness and distinctness of detail, and the learned and distinguished names connected with the scenes described are of such weight, that it is impossible to deny the conviction impressed upon the mind that either Spiritualism is one of the greatest delusions o the age, or that it is indeed a new manifestation of supernatural power, deserving the investigations of our theologians and teachers. The work, from its extreme interest, will amply repay a careful perusal."

The Boston Journal says, —
"Mr. Sargent has here collected a vast amount of information, and whoever wishes to have an intelligent epitome of the whole history of modern Spiritualism will find it in this volume."

For Sale by

COLBY AND RICH,

No. 9 Montgomery Place, Boston, Mass.

NOW READY.

A BIOGRAPHY

OF

MRS. J. H. CONANT,

The World's Medium of the Nineteenth Century.

A HISTORY OF HER MEDIUMSHIP

From Childhood to the Present Time:

BEING A NARRATIVE OF THE

Personal Experiences, Sharp Trials, and Liberalizing Victories achieved in the cause of Human Reason and Spiritual Knowledge.

––––––––

Let the heart-stricken read it, and be comforted;
Let the earth-weary peruse it, and be glad;
Let the world's workers explore it, and be encouraged;
Let the doubter scan its incontrovertible testimony, and be confounded;
Let the true man and woman, wherever abiding, recognize in it the life-line of a *kindred soul.*

COLBY AND RICH,

PUBLISHERS,
NO. 9 MONTGOMERY PLACE,
BOSTON, MASS.

FLASHES OF LIGHT

FROM

THE SPIRIT-LAND,

THROUGH THE MEDIUMSHIP OF

MRS. J. H. CONANT.

COMPILED AND ARRANGED BY

ALLEN PUTNAM,

Author of "Spirit-Works;" "Natty, a Spirit;" "Mesmerism, Spiritualism,
Witchcraft, and Miracle;" Etc., Etc.

———————•———————

This comprehensive volume of more than four hundred pages
will present to the reader a wide range of useful information
upon subjects of the utmost importance.

THE DISEMBODIED MINDS

of many distinguished lights of the past

HERE SPEAK

to the embodied intelligences of to-day, proclaiming their views
as derived from or modified by the FREEDOM FROM ARTIFICIAL
CONSTRAINT, and the ADDED LIGHT OF THE SPIRIT-
WORLD, concerning

THE ORIGIN OF MAN,

the duty devolving upon each individual, and the

DESTINY OF THE RACE.

As an Encyclopædia of Spiritual Information, this work is
without a superior.

———————•———————

Price $1.50.   Postage 22 cents.

———————•———————

COLBY AND RICH, PUBLISHERS,

9 Montgomery Place, Boston.

THE CLERGY

A

SOURCE OF DANGER

TO THE

AMERICAN REPUBLIC.

BY W. F. JAMIESON.

"By being a good Churchman, a person might become a bad citizen."
—*Fox's Speech in the House of Commons, Parl. Hist., Vol. xxix, p.* 1377.

"The king, [George III,] on every occasion, paid a court to the clergy."
"He was, therefore, sure of their support, and they zealously aided him in every attempt to oppress the Colonies."—*Buckle's History of Civilization in England, Vol. i, p.* 343.

"During almost a hundred and fifty years, Europe was afflicted by religious wars, religious massacres, and religious persecutions: not one of which would have arisen, if the great truth had been recognized, that the state has no concern with the opinions of men, and no right to interfere, even in the slightest degree, with the form of worship which they may choose to adopt.—*Buckle's History, p.* 190.

CLOTH - - - - - - - $1,50
GILT - - - - - - - 2,00
POSTAGE 20 CENTS.

ORIGIN AND PROGRESS

OF THE

MOVEMENT FOR THE

RECOGNITION OF THE

CHRISTIAN GOD, JESUS CHRIST

AND THE BIBLE,

IN THE

UNITED STATES CONSTITUTION.

BY W. F. JAMIESON.

PRICE 15 CENTS, POSTAGE 2 CENTS.

COLBY & RICH,

No. 9 MONTGOMERY PLACE,

BOSTON,

Publishers and Booksellers

KEEP A COMPLETE ASSORTMENT OF

SPIRITUAL, PROGRESSIVE, REFORM,

AND

MISCELLANEOUS BOOKS,

AT WHOLESALE AND RETAIL.

AMONG THE AUTHORS ARE, —

ANDREW JACKSON DAVIS, Judge J. W. EDMONDS,
Hon. ROBERT DALE OWEN, Prof. S. B. BRITTAN,
WILLIAM DENTON, ALLEN PUTNAM,
JAS. M. PEEBLES, EPES SARGENT,
HENRY C. WRIGHT, W. F. EVANS,
ERNEST RENAN, HUDSON TUTTLE,
GILES B. STEBBINS, A. B. CHILD,
WARREN CHASE, P. B. RANDOLPH,
D. D. HOME, WARREN S. BARLOW,
T. R. HAZARD, Rev. T. B. TAYLOR,
A. E. NEWTON, J. O. BARRETT,
Rev. M. B. CRAVEN, Rev. WM. MOUNTFORD.

Mrs. EMMA HARDINGE, Miss LIZZIE DOTEN,
Mrs. J. S. ADAMS, Mrs. MARIA M. KING,
ACHSA W. SPRAGUE, Mrs. L. MARIA CHILD,
BELLE BUSH, Mrs. LOIS WAISBROOKER.

TERMS CASH. — Orders for Books must be accompanied by all or part cash. When the money sent is not sufficient to fill the order, the balance must be paid C.O.D.

Any Book published in England or America, not out of print, will be sent by mail or express.

☞ Catalogues of Books giving prices, &c., sent free.

BANNER OF LIGHT:

AN EXPONENT OF THE

SPIRITUAL PHILOSOPHY

OF THE NINETEENTH CENTURY.

PUBLISHED WEEKLY

AT 9 MONTGOMERY PLACE, . . . BOSTON, MASS.

LUTHER COLBY.   ISAAC B. RICH.

THE BANNER OF LIGHT is a first-class eight-page Family Newspaper, containing FORTY COLUMNS OF INTERESTING AND INSTRUCTIVE READING, classed as follows:

LITERARY DEPARTMENT. — Original Novelettes of reformatory tendencies, and occasionally translations from French and German authors.

REPORTS OF SPIRITUAL LECTURES — By able Trance and Normal Speakers.

ORIGINAL ESSAYS — Upon Spiritual, Philosophical, and Scientific Subjects.

EDITORIAL DEPARTMENT. — Subjects of General Interest, the Spiritual Philosophy. Current Events, Entertaining Miscellany, Notices of New Publications, &c.

MESSAGE DEPARTMENT. — A page of Spirit-Messages from the departed to their friends in earth-life, given through the mediumship of MRS. J. H. CONANT, proving direct spirit-intercourse between the Mundane and Super-Mundane Worlds.

All which features render this journal a popular Family Paper, and at the same time the Harbinger of a Glorious Scientific Religion.

TERMS OF SUBSCRIPTION IN ADVANCE:

Per Year, $3.00....Six Months, $1.50....Three Months, 75 Cts.

In remitting by mail, a Post Office Order or Draft on Boston or New York payable to the order of COLBY AND RICH, is preferable to Bank Notes, since, should the Order or Draft be lost or stolen, it can be renewed without loss to the sender. Subscriptions discontinued at the expiration of the time paid for.

Subscribers in Canada will add to the terms of subscription 20 cents per year, for pre-payment of American postage

Specimen Copies sent Free

ADVERTISEMENTS inserted at twenty cents per line for the first, and fifteen cents per line for each subsequent insertion

All communications intended for publication, or in any way connected with the Editorial Department should be addressed to the EDITOR. Letters to the Editor, not intended for publication, should be marked "private" on the envelope.

COLBY & RICH,

PUBLISHERS AND BOOKSELLERS,

No. 9 Montgomery Place, Boston, Mass.,

KEEP FOR SALE ALL

Spiritual, Progressive and Reform Publications.

For Prices, &c , see Catalogues, and advertisements in the Banner of Light.